THE Marriage *OF* True Minds

THE Marriage

OF

True Minds

STEPHEN EVANS

UNBRIDLED
BOOKS

This is a work of fiction.
The names, characters, places
and incidents are either the product of the author's
imagination or are used fictitiously, and any resemblance
to actual persons living or dead, business
establishments, events, or locales is entirely coincidental.

Unbridled Books
Denver, Colorado

Library of Congress Cataloging-in-Publication Data

Evans, Stephen, 1955–
The marriage of true minds / Stephen Evans.
p.   cm.
ISBN 978-1-932961-46-1 (trade pbk.)
1. Lawyers—Fiction.   2. Divorced people—Fiction.   3. Animal
rights activists—Fiction.   4. Minneapolis (Minn.)—Fiction.   I. Title.
PS3605.V377M37 2008
813'.6—dc22

2008000552

1   3   5   7   9   10   8   6   4   2

Book design by SH · CV

First Printing

He laughed to free his mind from his mind's bondage.

—JAMES JOYCE

THE Marriage *OF* True Minds

CHAPTER 1

Alteration

MINNEAPOLIS STAR-TRIBUNE, June 11

Local barrister Nicholas Ward was arrested yesterday for releasing more than 100 live lobsters into the indoor pool at the mayor's mansion in Minneapolis.

Mr. Ward, formerly a prominent environmental attorney and founding partner of the local firm Ward and Grant, allegedly persuaded 12 Minneapolis grocery stores to donate the lobsters by claiming that the crustaceans were the rightful property of endangered Hawaiian monk seals. The seals, Mr. Ward reportedly explained, are currently on the endangered species list because humans are stealing their lobsters.

At Mr. Ward's request, Department of Public Works employees filled the mayor's pool with non-chlorinated saltwater and more than 100 blocks of ice. Unnamed sources at the department confirmed that Mr. Ward convinced them the mayor was having a beach party. The ice, he claimed, represented the effects of global warming on arctic populations.

Once the lobsters were safely deposited in the mayor's pool,

Mr. Ward summoned the media. During the ensuing lecture, he defended his actions by citing at length numerous obscure judicial precedents. He then made his getaway in a chauffeured stretch limousine, accompanied by a gray-and-white sheepdog puppet.

No charges have been filed, pending a psychiatric evaluation.

CHAPTER 2

Impediments

After the divorce, Lena had thought Nick was just going through an understandable period of mourning. She had been certain he would snap out of it eventually. And he had, just not in the way anyone had expected.

Lena stepped alone onto an elevator in the Wells Fargo Building in downtown Minneapolis. For forty-four floors, visions of ambulances, fire departments, and SWAT teams danced in her head. She had been out of town for three days. That was more than enough time for disaster to strike again.

On the forty-fifth floor, Lena rushed out of the elevator and sped down the corridor. At the end of the hallway, she stopped and performed her ritual invocation, running her fingers across the raised letters on the sign:

WARD AND GRANT
ATTORNEYS AT LAW

She dashed past the reception area and fled into her private office without speaking to her assistant, Sharon, who quickly followed her in.

The office furniture was a cool mixture of glass and steel, with several small exceptions: on the shelves behind the desk, stuffed animals roamed a law-book jungle. Most were elephants, ranging from just a few inches in height to nearly a foot.

Lena moved behind her desk and sat, gripping the cool edge with both hands, steadying herself for the news.

"Welcome back," Sharon began.

"Just tell me," Lena replied.

"How was the conference?"

"Just tell me."

"I'm glad to see you too."

The desktop surface was one of a kind: antique Veronese crystal, six feet long, three feet wide, and one inch thick. Clear glass pillars six inches in diameter supported each corner. At sunset on high-summer evenings, the light swept through the floor-to-ceiling windows at just the right angle, refracting in the crystal edge, spectral shards blossoming across the office walls and ceiling.

Lena never kept anything on the desk.

"Just tell me."

Sharon consulted her notes for dramatic effect, violet eyes highlighted in the reflection from the desk.

"You got calls from a chauffeur, twelve grocery stores, CNN, and the mayor."

Lena paused for a moment, evaluating the news, correlating the results. At least it wasn't an ambulance or the fire department or the SWAT team. She marshaled her energy, closed her eyes, then exhaled her mantra: *WhyMe.*

"Anything business-related?"

"Harrison Cross and the Luria gang confirmed for one o'clock."

"Good. Call the grocery stores and give them my credit-card number. Get me the mayor now."

As Sharon left the room, Lena pulled a worn notebook from the credenza behind her and flipped back in search of a blank page. To a stranger, the scribbled notes would have communicated only haste and emotional duress. Not even Sharon could decipher them. But the doodles in the margins comprised a hieroglyphic record of postmarital dissolution:

Page 1: A heart with an arrow through it.

Page 10: A heart with two arrows through it.

Page 50: No heart. Lots of arrows.

Page 100: A hairy, dog-like creature.

Page 150: *AAAAAAAAAAAHHHHHHHHHHHHHHHH!!!!!!!!!!!*

She had turned a few more pages and found a blank one but had not yet begun to write when the phone rang. She swung around in her chair, stared at the device on the credenza. Again and again the noise tingled in her brain like a sweet electrocution. Finally it stopped.

Sharon poked her head into the office.

"The mayor's office is on line one."

Lena donned the wireless headset like a tiara of thorns, then punched a button.

"Lena Grant for the mayor. Yes, I'll hold."

Lena could not imagine a sequence of events that connected a chauffeur, twelve grocery stores, a cable news network, and the mayor. But she knew who could.

"Hello, Mayor, it's Lena, I'm surprised to—"

Lena stopped. Her eyes widened, then narrowed.

"Where did he get that much salt? Oh. Yes, I suppose it does look bad when road salt intended for public safety ends up in the swimming pool of an elected official. I promise I will talk to him. Thank you, Mayor. I'll see you at the fund-raiser next week."

Lena had to find Nick.

She could try his cell phone. But either he didn't remember to carry it or he didn't remember how to retrieve messages or he did remember but wouldn't. Or maybe it was just her messages he ignored.

Lena paced in front of her office windows. If she looked straight down, the height still made her uneasy. If she looked out over the city, her eyes were inevitably drawn to the southwestern part of Minneapolis, where Lake of the Isles lay hidden behind neighborhood hills. The lake also made her uneasy. The area had become Nick's favorite haunt. When she had to find him, it was always her first stop.

If Nick wasn't at the lake, holding vigil with the squirrels or marshaling the geese or communing with the Norway pines or whatever it was he did there, she could try his condo about two blocks away. She had bought the place for him after the divorce, hoping he would enjoy having a home near the lake. She had liked the feel of the place, the streaky light morning and afternoon, the old whitewashed stucco walls and the burnished wooden floor. It seemed healthy, and that was what he needed, she thought. But the neighbors informed her that he mostly used the apartment for storage. What he had to store she didn't want to know.

If he wasn't at the condo, then the bank on Lake Street would be her next stop. Nick ventured into the branch at unpredictable intervals, withdrawing large amounts of cash that apparently lasted him for months.

She had opened the account after the divorce, when she had borrowed enough to buy out Nick's share of the law firm. Nick had more or less absconded from life during that period, so Lena and Nick's sister, Grace, a real estate broker who lived in Phoenix, were also listed on the account, just in case. Lena visited the bank every once in a while to educate a new branch manager about Nick. When she had last checked, there had still been a quarter of a million dollars in the account.

Sharon interrupted the planning for Lena's expedition.

"You have a call."

"I'm not here," Lena pleaded. "Unless it's an ambulance. Or the fire department. Or the SWAT team."

Sharon paused to get it right.

"It's your ex-sister-in-law."

Lena retrieved the headset, walked back to her desk, flipped open the well-doodled notebook.

"Hi, Grace. We're meeting with—what?"

As she listened, Lena once more silently reenacted her personal psychodrama: *AAAAAAAAAAAHHHHHHHHHHHHHH!!!!!!!!!!!*

"Where is he?"

She wrote: "GVPI 9021" and sighed

"Okay. I've got it. I'll be in touch."

Lena once again ripped off the headset and sent it flying into space. Then she donned her sunglasses, snared her briefcase (hefting it to make sure it possessed the proper density), and strode briskly into the office corridor. Sharon was playing a noisy game on her computer.

"You know, this Luria game is fun."

For a few seconds, Lena was caught up watching the game. A

knight in rusty armor struggled alone across a treacherous moat while battling demon slime rats with a glowing lance to reach a haunted castle where a legendary treasure was concealed.

It all seemed vaguely familiar.

"I'm going to hell," Lena announced.

Sharon didn't lift her head from the screen.

"I'll forward your messages."

Lena's Carmon Red Porsche convertible flared into the parking lot of the Golden Valley Psychiatric Institute, halting just before impaling the "Visitors Only" sign. She thrust the car door too wide, grabbed her briefcase, and hugged it to her breast like an umpire's chest guard.

She closed her eyes and took two long breaths.

When she opened them again, her focus drifted up to the top floor of the nine-story white building, then down the long row of barred windows.

Lena marched up the daisy-lined path and through the revolving glass doors. She entered the reception area in fullback mode, swinging her aluminum briefcase when necessary like a mirrored wrecking ball. The receptionist greeted her with "Please sign" but didn't quite get the "in" out before Lena was in the elevator.

On the ninth floor, an attendant sat reading a comic book, his orange-sneakered feet contrasting with the tiny white desk on which they rested. As Lena approached, he jammed the book into the pocket of his white lab coat and stood, apparently aiming for cool but willing to settle for official. Lena guessed he'd been on the job only a few weeks.

She stared expectantly at the attendant. Under her implacable yet marginally amused gaze, he fiddled with his bright orange Tweety Bird tie, reminding her of a beagle bravely wagging its tail at the veterinarian. After deciding that nothing was likely to happen in the near future without some form of communication, Lena gave in.

"Nicholas Ward."

"Oscar," replied Oscar.

Lena had a daily threshold of vexation beyond which any additional exasperation began to seem funny. In the face of enormous irritation, she would sometimes begin to giggle uncontrollably. She had already passed the vexation threshold but was successfully suppressing the nervous response, which made her face turn brittle and her eyes squint slightly. Oscar began to puddle under her stare. Lena came to his rescue.

"I'm here to see Nick Ward. He's in room 9021."

"And you are?" Oscar asked.

"Busier than you."

"That's a broad category."

Lena's smile burst through but was quickly withdrawn.

"Follow me," Oscar said, more question than command.

He unlocked the double steel doors, and she followed him through and down a long white corridor in which only the numbers differentiated one room from another.

"Why is everything white?" Lena asked.

"Don't know. Maybe it shows the clean better," Oscar replied.

"I think people would prefer some color."

"This place has been here for a hundred years. Maybe back then they didn't think of patients as people."

Lena glanced at the comic book hanging out of his pocket. The cover was torn in half, and the staples holding the pages together were gone.

"I didn't mean to interrupt your reading," she said.

Oscar reached down and drew out the rumpled book.

"Doctor Strange has just entered the mystical dimension and is battling his archnemesis Baron Mordo with the All-Seeing Eye of Agamotto."

"That one looks like someone slept on it," Lena noted.

"A comic book in mint condition is an offense against the multiverse. I only collect damaged comics with torn covers and missing pages."

"Me too," Lena replied.

Oscar gently turned a few pages.

"There's no telling what you can learn from comics."

"No telling," Lena agreed.

Oscar halted at a door at the end of the corridor and raised up on tiptoe to look in the window. Then he unlocked the door, braced his weight on the handles, and, lifting his feet, rode the door open.

Quickly filling the open passage, Lena scanned the tiny enclosure. The room was small and rectangular. A neatly made single bed lined the wall to the left. A tiny dull-white table and upright wooden chair stood against the right wall, leaving a small space in front of the barred shatterproof window. There was no mirror, no decoration, no place for personal items.

At first Lena didn't see the puppet sitting on the bed, braced upright by a pillow, almost invisible on the bland bed coverings. When she had first seen him years before, twenty-four inches of soft fake fur had gleamed white amid patches of gray. Now he reminded her of a disheveled furry Buddha, his gray coat matted, wisps of ash-colored hair spilling over his forehead. Well, it happened to everyone else, she thought, why not him?

Finally she looked at Nick. As usual, she had the odd sensation that she was seeing him for the first time, as if she had never met him before. He was always taller than she remembered. And thinner, she thought. He always looked thinner. Of course the straitjacket he was wearing emphasized his lanky frame, rough cloth tapering from broad shoulders to slim waist, reminding her of a human cyclone, as though at any minute he might sweep the room into chaos. She noted the effect, wondering how she could re-create it in her own wardrobe.

Nick wheeled his entire taut body around in baby steps.

"Quick! Hide!" he warned the reclining moppet.

Lena was not amused.

"Take it off," Lena ordered. Oscar jumped.

"Excuse me?"

"The jacket," she said. "Take it off."

Oscar started to peel off his lab coat. Lena, patience not quite working into a smile, explained: "Not yours. His."

Oscar glanced at Nick and assumed a worried expression. Lena guessed that removing straitjackets was beyond his charter.

"Restraints are hospital policy with new patients who are potentially violent," Oscar contended.

Lena swung her briefcase in a blurry arc into the steel door. An ominous thud reverberated down the white-tiled hall.

"The question is not," Lena informed Oscar without taking her eyes from Nick, "whether *he* is going to hurt *me*."

Oscar walked quickly over to Nick and removed the straitjacket. Then he took off his own coat just in case.

Nick tilted his head, a look no one but Lena could decode. She flashed her dark lashes in mock Morse code response.

"You want me to stay just in case?" Oscar asked with concern.

"That won't be necessary," Lena assured him.

"Actually, I was talking to him."

Lena turned to Oscar with renewed appreciation, which he appeared to interpret (correctly) as a mild threat.

"I'll leave now," Oscar added quickly.

Lena smiled her approval. Oscar mouthed the word *Sorry* to Nick as he closed the door.

Lena laid her briefcase on the small table and sat on the bed. She waited without speaking.

Lena always waited for Nick to speak first. It was her only way of knowing which Nick she would be dealing with. She had come to think of his pantheon of moods as different people, in the tactical rather than psychosocial sense. She had in her mind isolated twelve different Nicks, all undeniably Nickish though she could never quite determine what core element linked them all together. Like a shattered mirror that retained in the shards the final image before the catastrophe, bits and pieces of Nick flashed out but the whole was chaos.

"Well," said Nick finally, "look what the sharks dragged in."

She sighed internally with relief, hoping she recognized ironic, slightly acrimonious ex-husband Nick. She could at least talk with him, maybe even convince him of the trouble he was in.

"I told you I'd always be there for you," Lena responded.

"Yeah, but then you threw me out."

"I meant I'd be there for you as long as you weren't there for me."

Nick rubbed his arms and wrists to restore the circulation.

"What are you doing here?" he asked.

"Your sister called me."

"Grace from Grace."

"I'm defending you."

Nick picked up the puppet and held him close.

"And me without my belt and shoelaces," he lamented.

"Want mine?"

"Always the humanitarian. Say hi to Sancho," Nick said, holding the puppet out to her.

"Hello, Sancho," Lena said with more genuine sweetness than she intended. "We need to get him cleaned up. He's gotten a little dingy."

"Manufacturer's instructions: Clean with a mild soap and damp cloth. Do not dry clean—the fumes make him sneeze. Do not microwave—he is not zucchini. Do not blow dry—he looks like he just stuck his head out of a speeding car."

Lena readjusted the atmosphere by opening her briefcase and shielding herself with papers.

"Nick, you do understand how serious this is?"

"You're just after my money."

"I have money."

"Can you lend me some?"

"Do you know where you are?" Lena asked.

Nick countered with Irving Berlin.

"Heaven, I'm in heaven," he crooned.

He pulled a reluctant Lena to her feet, wove his arm around her waist, and began waltzing around the room. In even modest heels, she looked him in the eyes; over the years she had learned to see more in them than he wanted her to. She thought. Though she could never really be sure what he wanted. Now his eyes danced along with his voice, but slightly ahead, as though hearing the sound before she did. It was confusing: eyes then voice then motion. She averaged them out in her mind, but followed the motion to keep from falling.

"And my heart beats so that I can hardly speak," he sang in a throaty baritone she remembered well.

"This is not a waltz," Lena admonished.

"And I seem to find the happiness I seek," Nick crooned.

"It's in four-four time."

"When we're out together dancing cheek to cheek to cheek."

Lena stepped back.

"Why do I do this?" she asked Sancho.

"I'm magnetic," Nick explained. "Exotic. Quixotic!"

Lena stuffed the papers back in her briefcase.

"And what do those words have in common?"

Nick pondered, then ventured: "-ic?"

"Exactly."

Lena knocked loudly on the door.

"Let me out," she pleaded.

"Practice makes perfect," Nick explained to Sancho.

Lena swung around. Nick ducked.

"Why did you dump lobsters in the mayor's pool?" she asked, curiosity overcoming her urge to flee.

"Two reasons," Nick replied, morphing into the persona Lena had nicknamed the Thin Man, the detective elucidating the modus operandi in the final reel. The persona had often been an advantage in a law partner, but was a disadvantage in a husband, and extremely frustrating in an ex.

"No politician will condemn animals to death on national television."

"National television?"

"Lobsters in the mayor's pool make for exceptional video. I have CNN on speed dial."

"Why lobsters?" Lena asked.

"They were depressed. The blank antennae. The listless mandibles. The lack of interest in everyday scuttling."

Lena sighed.

"Do you want to see the secret sign of the International Brotherhood of Crustaceans?" he asked.

Without waiting for an answer, he placed his fist to his forehead, extended his index and middle fingers, and wiggled them.

Lena ran a hand through her Porsche-blown hair.

"What is the mayor supposed to do with a hundred lobsters?" she asked, certain she did not want to know the answer, or at least not Nick's answer.

"One hundred and forty-four," Nick corrected. "I have it all taken care of. I donated two hundred and fifty thousand dollars to the Marine Education Center at the Minnesota Zoo to fund a lobster exhibit. The tanks will be ready in a week, and the mayor will reap loads of publicity at the opening. We just need to send lots of ice in the meantime."

Lena's eyes flared. That was all of the money he had. All of which she had borrowed to pay him. All of which she had struggled to finally pay off only a few months before.

"Nick! Are you nuts?"

"Hmmm. Let's examine the evidence," he said, picking up the straitjacket.

"No. I mean. You can't afford that! What are you going to do? This is a very bad plan."

Nick looked at her and smiled.

"I don't make plans. I have visions."

Lena paused, struggling to catch up.

"Why ice?"

"Lobsters prefer a water temperature of forty to forty-five degrees Fahrenheit."

"But."

"If only you had seen the facets of relief, even hope, reflected in their grateful eyestalks."

Lena shook her head.

"Nick. How do you expect to live?"

He paused. She hated when he paused because it gave her time to hope. Then he started singing.

"E come vivo? Vivo!"

Lena growled inwardly. His familiar mélange of mysterious amusement and ironic compassion always forced her into momentary doubt, no matter how certain she was that she was right. Yet she smiled in spite of herself that he remembered her favorite opera.

"Tu sol comandi, amor," she replied.

Oscar swung open the door.

"It's good to see you again," Nick whispered as Lena brushed by him. A breathtaking plummet into heartsickness stopped her, turned her slowly back to him.

"It's good to see you too, Nick. But you have to understand. I can't do this anymore."

Nick glanced past her at Oscar.

"Actually, I was talking to him."

Lena and Oscar walked in silence down the hospital corridor, until Oscar finally asked: "So what's the deal with him?"

"What do you mean?"

"Is he dangerous?"

"Are you planning to marry him?"

"No."

"Then you're safe."

They began to walk again, the only sound Lena's heels tip-clacking down the spotted white linoleum that had been all the rage in asylum corridors fifty years earlier.

"Who is his doctor?" Lena asked.

"Richardson. Second floor. Good guy."

"Thanks."

"So what's wrong with him?"

Lena paused, replaying as she did each night the years of turbulence to see if the possibility of a conclusion could be found. Finally she dangled a set of keys before Oscar's eyes.

"You figure that out, you can have my Porsche."

"Deal," Oscar agreed.

The congenial comfort of the second floor contrasted with the forced courtesy of the first and the blank efficiency of the ninth. Lena wandered down the unpretentious hallway for a few moments before locating the office of Dr. Henry Richardson. She knocked on the door and entered.

A heavyset man of medium height sat, eyes closed, behind an uncluttered desk. Music was playing. Piano. Chopin. A nocturne.

"Dr. Richardson?"

"Yes?" replied the man, not moving or even opening his eyes. His hands were lightly clasped, as if he were meditating or praying or making a pronouncement from the bench.

"My name is Lena Grant. I'm an attorney representing Nicholas Ward. He is being held here."

The doctor opened his eyes and focused on her for the first time.

"Mr. Ward has been admitted," the doctor corrected her. "I spoke to his sister yesterday."

Lena glanced around at the furnishings. Something was missing, something she expected to see but didn't. She couldn't put her finger on what it might be.

"Grace called me."

"Please sit down," said the doctor, indicating two chairs in front of his desk. Lena sat in one of them. The doctor came around the desk and sat in the other.

"He was brought in last night," the doctor continued. "Someone at the precinct knew him—"

"He's an attorney also," Lena stated. "I mean he was."

"We administered one hundred milligrams of Thorazine, which kept him sedated most of the night."

"Thorazine?"

"An antipsychotic drug. We administer Thorazine to inhibit delusions or hallucinations. Right now he seems relatively functional, so we are giving him lithium for mood stabilization."

"He wouldn't hurt anyone," she stated.

"He may not intend to hurt anyone," the doctor corrected her.

Lena sat back and took a moment to absorb the information.

"Have you known him long?" the doctor asked.

"He was one of my professors in law school. And we were partners in a law firm."

"I see."

"And we were married."

The doctor looked up, moved back around to the other side of the desk, and began taking notes.

"How long ago was the divorce?"

"Almost two years ago."

"Any kids?"

"No. We. No."

"May I ask why you got divorced?"

"Why? I mean, why are you asking why?"

"Don't worry. I don't date lawyers," the doctor assured her.

"You're smart."

"Yes, I am. Is there any family history of mental illness?"

"He drove me crazy. Does that count?"

The doctor smiled. Lena shook her head.

"No," she continued. "Not that I know of. I mean. No. Doctor, are you telling me that there's something seriously wrong with him?"

Dr. Richardson got up, walked back around the desk, and sat again in the chair next to Lena.

"Do you mind?" he asked, pulling out a cigar. Lena shook her head. "It's against the law and hospital rules. But sometimes . . ."

She nodded, but his need for it made her nervous. He clipped one end of the cigar, lit the other, inhaled, and blew the smoke away from her. Then he extinguished it and chewed the smoldering cylinder.

"You know what a delusion is?" he asked.

"I told you I was married," Lena replied.

The doctor's smile flashed again, then faded quickly.

"From a psychiatric perspective, a delusion is a false belief that the patient maintains in spite of substantial contrary evidence. While it's too soon yet for a definitive diagnosis, I believe Mr. Ward has what we would call delusional disorder."

"Is that serious?"

"It can be. The neural activity, or brain function, in these cases is extraordinary. The French philosopher René Descartes once said: 'I think, therefore I am.' In a sense, your ex-husband thinks too much, so he isn't who he is."

Lena felt her heart beat rapidly as the fears that had grown slowly over the last few years coalesced inside her.

"Can it be treated?"

"Treatment can be effective in some cases. A combination of medication and therapy."

"You don't sound too encouraging"

The doctor relit the cigar, took another puff, and then put it out again.

"As I said, it's too soon. But there are unusual symptoms in your husband's case. The puppet, for instance. It's not uncommon for delusional patients to see an inanimate object as human, though this anthropomorphic behavior can take many forms.

"In most cases, when you challenge a delusion, the patient will be insistent, even to the point of violence. The unusual aspect of Mr. Ward's illness is that when you challenge his delusions, he readily acknowledges that they are fantasy. Yet out in the world, he behaves as though they were real. That's a conundrum."

Lena made a professional effort to smile. The result was brittle and unconvincing.

"Did the divorce cause this?" she asked.

The doctor's expression smoothed over.

"No. The biochemical and genetic mechanisms of the disorder would already have been in place. Most likely the illness would have manifested in time regardless. Did the stress of the divorce affect the progress of the disorder? Possibly. The resulting disruption could have precipitated the initial episode. But that does not mean that you were at fault."

"Doctor, I'm a lawyer. My business is identifying who's at fault. I know where the blame goes."

Dr. Richardson saluted her.

"I'm going to start sending my patients to you."

Lena sat up straight.

"There are no books here," she stated.

The doctor smiled.

"No books," he agreed.

"I expected books. Shelves and shelves of books. Is there a reason that you don't have books?"

"Yes," he said, adding nothing more.

"Okay. Well. I'm glad there's a reason."

The doctor leaned back in his chair.

"It must be nice to be in a job where you win once in a while," he said. "The best I ever seem to do is tie."

"The only victory in life is being a good loser," Lena replied.

"Who said that?"

"Somebody dead."

Preston Winter's desk always reminded Lena of a Bavarian castle. Case files stacked around the perimeter formed uneven battlements. A coffee-stain moat spread across the faded gray rug, evidence of sieges past. Lena entered the office without knocking and sat by the northwest turret.

"I hate paperwork," Preston said.

"Then you picked the right job," Lena responded. "Assistant state's attorneys never do paperwork."

Preston emitted a quasi-amused blurt.

"You're early," he said. "I thought we were meeting at the gym."

"I have a problem."

Preston peered at her.

"You divorced him."

"This is serious."

Preston leaned forward.

"Is he dead?" he asked.

"Don't."

"Sorry. Injured?"

Lena folded her arms, at the same time defending and enhancing her breasts, a masterwork of effective communication she had perfected in junior high.

"He's in Golden Valley," she continued.

"Psychiatric Institute," Preston completed. "And the problem is—what?"

Lena leaned in, slipped off his glasses, and held his eyes with hers.

"I need a favor."

Preston jumped up, almost tumbling Lena into the northeast spire, and gathered a stack of papers.

"I have a meeting."

Lena beat him to the door.

"It's Nick," she pleaded.

"Exactly," he answered harshly. "It's Nick. Stay out of it."

Preston brushed past her.

"I told him," Lena announced.

Preston froze in the doorway but didn't turn back.

"What did you tell him?"

"I told him," Lena said slowly, pulling him back to her, "that this is the last time. After this he's out of my life for good."

Preston sighed.

"I'll do what I can," he said.

"See you at the gym," she said. "Dinner afterward?"

"What are friends for?"

Sharon was standing outside the conference room doorway, holding a folder.

"Harrison Cross and his entourage are inside," she said.

Lena's eyes brightened. Eager to confront an adversary on whom she could profitably focus her frustration, she accepted the folder, constructed a smile, and strolled confidently into the room.

The decor in the conference room was casual but professional. Even the toy giraffe that poked its head through the silk tree in the corner wore thick horn-rimmed glasses.

Lena sat on the near side of the table. Across from her, a team of four attorneys conferred with quiet confidence. Sharon took her usual seat beside Lena.

Lena carefully laid the folder down on the conference table, then covered it with her hand. From across the polished mahogany divide, eight suspicious eyes peered down at the folder as the smug atmosphere cracked just a bit.

"I apologize for the delay," Lena began pleasantly.

"Ms. Grant, we have a flight to catch."

"Certainly, Mr. Cross. This won't take long," Lena reassured him.

Lena mentally reviewed Sharon's research on the man who sat across from her. Harrison Cross had been lead internal counsel for Luria Corporation since its formation in the early '80s. He had guided the transformation of the company into a collossus of entertainment software, pocketing not only a substantial corporate salary but also millions in stock options. Luria's new video game, Parzival II, scheduled for a holiday release, had received record advance orders. Cross seemed quite sure that neither he nor Luria had anything to fear from a boutique firm like Ward and Grant.

"The Luria Corporation illegally appropriated software designed by my client. All we are asking for is fair compensation."

Cross leered back at Lena.

"Ms. Grant, let me stop you there. I understand that this is not your standard practice area, so let me assure you that our settlement offer of fifty thousand dollars is more than generous, considering. Surely your client could use that money for her college education."

Cross leaned back in his chair. His three cronies followed suit. Lena sensed their confidence: they were going to be able to buy their way out of this cheaply. Even if Luria had appropriated the code illegally, they reckoned the court proceedings would bankrupt the tiny opposition firm long before a final verdict was rendered.

Cross explained: "Even if you win in court, I remind you that the appeals process alone could take ten years. Is your client prepared to wait that long? Are you?"

Lena didn't answer. She stood up hesitantly and moved to the corner. She knew that Cross would presume she did so to hide the defeat in her eyes.

Lena petted the giraffe, then straightened the eyeglasses that had fallen down over its elongated snout. Facing out the window, she said: "You are correct. This is not an area in which I often practice. I agreed to meet with you because the client is my ex-husband's niece. So this a family matter. Of sorts. And my client can wait as long as necessary. But as for me . . ."

Lena turned and smiled again. As she moved gracefully back to the conference table, something crystallized in her eyes. She leaned across the table and added in her most pleasant voice: "I hate waiting. Sharon?"

Sharon thrust the folder toward Cross, who stared at it but didn't move to touch it, as though he knew the folder was legal toxic waste.

"This is a motion for a temporary injunction preventing your company from selling any electronic gaming software in the United States. I plan to file this injunction in federal court today."

Cross stared hard at the folder, then responded dismissively: "You can't win."

"I don't have to win," she said with a shrug. "I just have to file."

Cross did not respond. Lena positioned her hand palm down over the folder.

"Once this motion is filed, the market will conclude that your software might not be on the shelves at Christmas. Your stock price will fall to its knees like a two-dollar whore," she continued. "And I will make sure you get fucked."

On the opposite side of the conference table, babble erupted from four alarmed faces.

Lena sat down next to Sharon.

"After the emergency stockholders' meeting, I predict that the new board of directors will settle generously with my client and terminate each of you for gross incompetence."

For a moment, there was no sound, though Lena imagined the flutter of evaporating stock options. Then Cross said: "That's stock manipulation."

"I'm just defending the innocent."

"Is this supposed to intimidate me?"

"Now, you could sue," Lena reminded him. "However, the appeals process alone could take ten years."

Lena set her watch on the table. Eight anxious eyes followed the leisurely yet jubilant progression of the second hand:

One.

Two.

Three.

Four.

Five.

Six.

Seven.

Eight.

Nine.

Lena observed the lawyers pass Three in anger, Five in denial, Seven in bargaining, and Nine in a fusion of acceptance and financial exhaustion. Lena released them.

"Are you prepared to wait that long?" she added with concern.

Cross hid behind his legal pad.

"What do you want?" he blurted out finally.

"Two point five million plus future royalties."

He winced.

"We'll have to talk to our board of directors."

"Talk fast," Lena said.

The Luria cohorts filed out of the room, arguing with one another while texting discrete messages to their brokers. Sharon closed the door behind them and turned to Lena.

"I've never heard you use that kind of language before."

"It's a matter of fairness," Lena replied. "We have a responsibility to communicate in a way they will understand."

Sharon nodded.

"You know, it was sort of a mixed metaphor."

"Well, it's not my standard practice area."

Lena offered the mysterious folder to Sharon.

"What's really in this?" Sharon asked.

Lena balanced the folder carefully in her hand.

"My guess is two million plus."

Sharon accepted the precious repository.

"Is this my bonus?"

Lena's smile didn't fade until she was midway into her office, when she saw the waiting stack of messages. The elephants saluted her with upraised trunks.

Lena lay on her back with her legs splayed wide. The fact that she was doing this in public was slightly embarrassing, abnormally irritating, and numbingly familiar.

She stared at the gym ceiling, forcing the weights up over and over while pondering Greek mythology. The names Sisyphus and Tantalus hovered in her sweat-induced haze. She couldn't remember which was which. And this annoyed her.

One of them was always thirsty, bound in a lake from which he couldn't drink. The other was always weary, condemned to push a boulder up a mountain forever; when he got almost to the top, it would roll down again. It occurred to her that if the one on the mountain freed the one in the lake, they could roll the boulder up together, then go down and get a drink.

Men, she thought. Never knew when to ask for help.

Lena closed her eyes and listened to the noises around her. Grunting, groaning, sighing, and puffing merged into a purgatory of uneasy flesh. And then she saw that it was not just in this room, but all through the city, the country, the world, every activity performed day in day out was just a variant of lying on your back with your legs spread wide, mindlessly pumping up and down. Then the ultimate solution flashed into her mind: Juice.

My blood sugar must be low, she thought.

Suddenly Preston Winter's face loomed over her.

"Hello, Pressssston," she grunted as she pressed the bar as high as she could.

Preston grunted in response, which made her laugh and almost lose control of the bar. He was standing at her head, looking down at her, which her visual orientation converted into hanging from the ceiling.

"Get down from there," she said crossly.

"The mayor?"

She had never looked at his face upside down before. Somehow the hemispheric perfection that anointed his football-hero looks in the everyday world was not sustained when that world was topsy-turvy. His eyebrows were crooked. Or was that because he was frowning?

"Preston?"

"The mayor!"

Lena reached up and centered his face over hers. It was bad enough that he was hanging from the ceiling, but did he have to be a bobblehead too?

"It's my case now. I hope you're happy," he said.

Lena grabbed his hand.

"Drop the charges. We'll agree to counseling and community service."

"He's nuts," Preston muttered. Lena wriggled out from under the bar and sat up.

"I can't let him go to jail."

Preston moved in front of her and sat on the bench, edging her thighs outward, his back to her. Lena slid her arms around him, easily encircling his chest, and sighed.

Preston covered her sweaty arms with his and inhaled deeply, pressing his polyester-plated back into the spandex-delimited cushion of her chest, interrupting her sigh with his own.

"Counseling and community service. And he stays on medication. The arraignment is tomorrow."

She kissed his neck.

"Thank you. I'll tell him tonight."

She rested her head against his shoulder.

"This is a nightmare," she said.

Preston twisted around.

"He is a nightmare. You need to wake up."

Lena and Oscar stood outside the door to Nick's hospital room, rapt in a silence that hovered just this side of distress. Inside the room, Nick was marching around the tiny space with Sancho on his arm.

Down and back.

Over the bed.

Up the chair.

Across the table.

It was better than a treadmill, Lena decided.

Given the specific choreography of leaps and gyrations, Lena guessed that they were parading to Nick's favorite: "The Liberty Bell" march by John Philip Sousa. He knew by heart each piccolo trill and trumpet flourish. Actual music was superfluous, apparently, since the only sound in the room was the patter of Nick's bare feet.

Oscar moved close to Lena.

"They're good."

"Practice makes perfect," Lena sighed.

Oscar opened the door. Nick crashed down on the bed as if playing fantasy musical chairs.

"At ease, soldier," Lena said as she stepped warily through the opening.

"Your husband is a very lucky man," Nick announced proudly.

"I don't have a husband."

"Then he's a very lucky man," Oscar muttered.

Lena turned to Oscar, able to summon irritation but not anger. "I heard that," she said.

Nick looked around her, smiling at Oscar.

"She did, too," Nick confirmed. "Don't ask me how."

Oscar shoved his hands in the pockets of his white coat.

"I meant that he's a very lucky man ever to have had the remarkable good fortune of . . ."

"Leave now," Lena said.

"While you can," Nick added.

Lena waited until the door closed and then walked to the window. It was late, only a few cars left in the parking lot. Her car was visible from the window. She wondered if Nick had seen her arrive, whether the marching was for her benefit.

She had seen him march before. Once, after a few glasses of champagne, she had even marched with him. It had been exhilarating. "Okay, here's the deal," she announced.

"How is Preston?" he asked.

"Preston is fine. The deal is they drop the charges without prejudice, which means—"

"I know what it means."

"Which means, if you violate the terms of the agreement, they can reinstate the charges. In return, in addition to general good behavior, you agree to medication, counseling—"

"Who do they want me to counsel?"

"And community service."

"Who do they want me to service?"

Lena glared.

Nick shrugged. "And if I refuse?"

"Then they'll order a psychiatric evaluation."

Sancho shuddered.

"They'll have a hearing."

A bigger shudder.

"And then they'll make a determination as to whether you are committed to a psychiatric ward or go to prison."

Sancho hid his head in Nick's shoulder.

"Can I think about it?" Nick asked. Lena ignored the request.

"The arraignment is tomorrow. No puppets."

Sancho looked around at her.

"He prefers 'Imaginary American,'" Nick explained.

Lena nodded apologetically and turned to leave. Then she felt a furry nudge on her shoulder. She turned back and found Sancho close enough to tickle her nose. Sancho's face moved aside to reveal Nick's unusually somber and genuine expression, like a souvenir of a lost adventure.

"We just wanted to say thanks," he said.

Her heart flashed. Lena had tamed her sadness, given it a home, taught it tricks (roll over, fetch, play dead), and made sure it would never run away. But occasionally it bounced up and surprised her.

"Amazing," she commented after a few seconds of intense interpretive effort convinced her that he was sincere. "You learned a new word."

As she reached for the door, Oscar swept it open from the outside.

"Everybody's learning," she said. "See you in court."

She did not look back.

Lena walked confidently into the hearing room. Her arrangement with Preston was approved. The paperwork was in perfect order. Nothing can go wrong, she thought—but nevertheless something would. She didn't know what, but she knew why.

The courtroom was small, with the judge's chambers directly behind the large wooden panel flanking the bench. To the right was the jury box (which was empty), to the left was the room where defendants were held before trial. About five feet in front of the bench were two long tables, one for the defense and one for the prosecution. A short wooden railing divided the court from the small gallery.

Nick was already sitting at the defendant's table playing tic-tactoe with Sancho. His restraints had been removed. Oscar was in the first row of the gallery, draped over the railing, alternately observing the game and reading an Iron Man comic book that might once have been the insole of someone's shoe.

Lena laid her briefcase on the table and stood looking down at the game.

"I said no puppets," Lena reminded Nick.

"Puppets? Where?" Nick asked as he and Sancho scanned the room.

Oscar leaned forward.

"Good luck in court today," he said.

"You should say, 'Break a leg,'" Nick replied.

"That's for the theater."

"Wherever I go, it's always theater."

Lena growled.

"People always tell me I look like Brad Pitt," Oscar said.

Both Nick and Lena swiveled to look at him.

"It's the eyes," Oscar explained.

Preston Winter entered the courtroom and took his place at the prosecutor's table. Nick and Sancho regarded him closely. Preston returned the dual stare for a few seconds, then shook his head at the pair. Sancho hid behind Lena, occasionally peeking around to see if Preston was watching, then ducking quickly out of sight.

Lena, still standing, faced Nick, laid her hand lightly on his shoulder, then dug her fingernails into his back as hard as she could.

"Cut it. Out," she commanded under a smile.

She sat down next to Nick at the table, spreading out her documents, noting peripherally that Nick was wearing his cherished dark-blue suit with the nearly invisible pinstripe that complemented the dark scarlet of her outfit. Suddenly and unexpectedly, she was engulfed by successive tidal waves of déjà vu and nostalgia and panic.

When they had decided to work together, Lena had not known what to expect, or how the dual aspect of their partnership would work. What she had not anticipated was the sense of transcendence, of gaining a context. She had learned to treasure that. And to mourn its loss.

Sitting next to Nick again alarmed Lena. She had not been in a courtroom with him since their last trial together as partners. He had neither contested nor acknowledged the divorce, except to sign the papers.

Lena ransacked her litigation case for an extra copy of the plea agreement and handed it to Nick.

"You might want to glance at this," she said and noticed that the document was trembling in her hand.

Nick smiled and settled down.

"Sure," he said and began to peruse the agreement.

The bailiff stood.

"All rise."

The judge walked briskly in and sat.

"Sit sit sit," she said.

Lena had never met Judge Anne Ritchfield, though they had attended some of the same political functions. Ritchfield was a rarity, a judge who had never practiced law. She had started as a psychiatric social worker, gotten her Ph.D. in clinical psychology at Emory University, and then attended law school at the University of St. Thomas while working as a child advocate. She had been appointed to a seat on the family court for Hennepin County, then elected to a seat on the Fourth Judicial District court for the State of Minnesota. She knew Preston well. Nick was unknown to her.

The judge scanned the courtroom quickly and gestured for the bailiff to approach.

"There is a stuffed animal on the defendant's table."

"Yes, Your Honor. I tried to take him away, but Mr. Ward claimed he's a material witness."

"And you just left it at that?"

"Yes, Your Honor."

The judge leaned over the bench and whispered: "What's the pool up to?"

The bailiff stuttered: "Uh. I. Twenty bucks."

"What was your guess?"

"That you'd confiscate it in under a minute."

"You lose. Call the case."

The bailiff paid the court reporter twenty dollars and declared: "State versus Nicholas Ward."

To which Nick replied, holding up the puppet: "Et al."

The judge ignored Nick. Lena glared at him, then stood.

"Elena Grant for the defense, Your Honor."

"Preston Winter for the state," Preston said, also standing.

Nick stood as well.

"Your Honor," he said, "if it please the court, we cite *Tahoe-Sierra Preservation Council, Inc., et al. v. Tahoe Regional Planning Agency et al.*, in which the court held that a regulation temporarily denying an owner all use of her property might not constitute a taking if the denial is part of the state's authority to enact safety regulations."

"What are you doing?" Lena interrupted.

"We have a responsibility to communicate in a way they will understand," Nick explained.

"Would you just let me do my job?"

Nick sat back down.

"Thank you, Mr. Ward," said the judge, "for that cogent yet completely irrelevant piece of information. I understand there is an agreement here," she continued, shuffling through documents.

"Yes, Your Honor," Preston and Lena said together, then smiled at each other.

The judge picked up the plea document and read for a few seconds.

"This agreement specifies one hundred sixty hours of community service."

"That is correct, Your Honor," Preston agreed.

"Plus mandatory counseling."

"That's also correct."

The judge flipped a page and threw Lena a quizzical glance.

"You're his ex-wife?"

"Yes, Your Honor."

"And his ex–law partner?"

"Yes."

Nick stood.

"Your Honor, the defense is willing to stipulate that counsel is ex-rated."

"Nick, sit down and shut up!" Lena ordered.

Nick sat.

"Counselor, what is going on?" the judge said.

"I'm representing the defendant. Today. Only," Lena explained.

"Today only."

"Sounds like a sale at K-Mart," Nick whispered to Sancho, and then Nick stood again.

"Your Honor," he said, "may I have a minute to confer with counsel?"

"Does the state object?" the judge asked.

"Yes, but go ahead," Preston said in a sulk.

"Make it fast, Mr. Ward."

Nick turned to Lena and got down on one knee.

"I imagine that I will love you for as long as we both shall live."

"Don't even think—" was all Lena got out before Nick stood, bent her back over the table, and kissed her, the rest trapped behind clenched lips as shock, panic, memory, and hormones fused with oxygen depletion.

"Thank you, Your Honor. No more questions," Nick announced, releasing Lena and sitting down just in time to avoid her flailing elbow.

The judge hefted the gavel as though contemplating whether to use it or toss it.

"Ms. Grant," she ordered in her sternest voice, "please control the defendant."

"Your Honor," said Lena, "that's not a case, it's a career."

Nick stood again.

"Your Honor, for the record, I'd just like to point out that technically I am not the defendant, since I have not yet been arraigned on the charges."

"Thank you, Mr. Ward," said the judge. "And I would like to point out that technically I am the one who decides whether you will be a defendant."

Nick considered.

"Your point is better than mine."

He sat down again. Lena muttered to him:

"What are you—"

Again Nick stood.

"However, since I am still an officer of the court, I feel it's my responsibility to point out that there is no provision in this agreement for supervision."

Lena and Preston exchanged expressions of chagrin. Nick was right. The judge glared at Preston.

"Is that correct, Mr. Winter?"

"No, Your Honor. I mean, yes, Your Honor, that is correct."

"Is the state ready to accept responsibility for the unsupervised actions of this def— of the accused?"

Preston glanced at Lena as if to say: "You owe me."

"Yes, Your Honor."

The judge nodded, then shook her head.

"Well, this is an election year, and you are braver than I am. Is there a responsible party who can take charge of the accused and oversee the counseling and community service?"

Preston and Lena both spoke at once: "Your Honor."

Then Preston continued: "I really don't think supervision will be necessary in this case."

"Well, I do. Is there a responsible party or not?"

"Your Honor, the defendant is—"

Lena glared at Nick, searching frantically for options that would keep him out of a psych ward or a jail.

Then she saw it.

She had seen it so often before. Yet the moment of recognition still captivated her.

Events simplified.

Intentions clarified.

And out of the frantic chaotic mystery, the hidden objective was achieved.

In the courtroom, she had seen it time and again. Always it was magical when Nick's rambling antics stood revealed—too late to act but not too late to appreciate—as reality unfolded at his command, the World According to Nick. All that was left to her, to anyone, was to play the destined part.

Lena stood and announced: "I'll do it."

"No fucking way!" Preston shouted.

"Counselor!" the judge admonished.

Lena looked back at Preston, shrugging while asking for sympathy she knew she would not get.

"Your Honor, there isn't anyone else," she explained. "No local relatives. No human friends."

She turned back to Nick.

"I'm all he has."

His innocent eyes infuriated her.

"And he knows it."

The judge turned her attention to Lena.

"Ms. Grant, are you sure you know what you're doing?"

"Yes, Your Honor. But I'm going to do it anyway."

The judge nodded.

"Very well," she said. "He's all yours. Amend the order and I'll sign it. Next case."

Lena ran to Preston, trying to explain. Nick, impassive, watched them argue on the other side of the courtroom. Oscar walked up behind Nick and picked up the puppet.

"Speaking of breaking a leg, I think she's going to break yours."

Preston cut off his conversation with Lena and stomped over to Nick.

"If you even breathe on her improperly, I will make it my life's mission to put you away permanently."

Lena flashed up to him. The words snapped out with chilling precision: "Wait. Till. I. Get. You. Home."

She whirled away and marched out of the courtroom.

Hand in hand with Sancho, Nick followed her through the polished swinging doors.

CHAPTER 3

Time's Fool

She graduated from Princeton with a B.A. in developmental neurolinguistics. Her undergraduate thesis examined the effect of the Dick and Jane series of children's readers on the ventromedial prefrontal cortex. In the summer after graduation, she rigorously researched potential life strategies:

✓ Who she should be
✓ What she should do
✓ When she should begin
✓ Where she should live
✓ How she should start

In the process, she identified five cities in which she might want to reside and continue her education:

✓ Boston
✓ Seattle
✓ San Francisco
✓ Chicago
✓ Washington

Accordingly, she set forth on a mission. After spending several days in each city, she compiled a dossier, rating each according to the following factors:

- ✓ Professional
- ✓ Educational
- ✓ Cultural
- ✓ Historical
- ✓ Social

Eventually she settled on Minneapolis, though it wasn't on the original list and she had never been there. But she had a feeling about it, which was intensified by the fact that she hadn't liked one thing or another about each of the other cities she had actually visited. And the fifty-mile-long Grand Rounds bike path around the city was a definite plus. Biking was one of her lifelong passions.

Several areas of graduate study intrigued her, but after lengthy and prudent consideration, she decided to study law. After researching well-known Minnesota law firms, she discovered that they hired extensively from the University of Minnesota. So, though it was very late in the summer, she applied to the law school. She was amazed when they contacted her almost immediately and told her she had been accepted for the fall term. She soon moved to a little apartment off University Avenue and began life in the Middle North.

In her first year of law school, she learned that she enjoyed studying The Law (she always thought of it that way, as if it were a mystical entity or an embodiment of elemental forces). She had imagined that The Law would be cold and arithmetic in precision. Instead she found in it a reflection of human life both as it was, and as it could be, lived.

In her second year, she discovered that she might enjoy being a lawyer. The practice of The Law as she envisioned it required strategy supported by organization, argument supported by information, art supported by compensation. Both the challenge and the complexity appealed to her.

In her third year, she enrolled in a class in environmental law because she had heard that the instructor was funny. She was mildly curious how anyone could make such a subject amusing, and slightly annoyed that anyone would try.

The instructor was an adjunct professor who taught the course at night while maintaining a solo practice during the day. He was rumored to have a legendary memory for environmental jurisprudence, able to cite word-for-word case law on both the federal and state levels.

When he first breezed into the lecture room, she puzzled casually over his looks, the lanky frame in the impeccable blue suit contrasting with the unkempt hair and muddy hiking boots. How could so many disparate components be combined in such an attractive way? she wondered.

As the term progressed, she was surprised to find that the instructor began to interest her more and more. She was well aware of the dynamic of teacher and student, had occasionally indulged in it, and found that the interest usually disappeared quickly after the indulgence. She had also known other brilliant, accomplished, and attractive men. They tended to see the world as a reflection of themselves and expected the women in their lives to be the perfect mirror. This was not a role she enjoyed.

Most of all, it was the instructor's combination of passion and humor that fascinated her. After class, he would sit in the front row of the lecture hall, usually just a few empty seats away, and talk genially about whatever legal conundrum intrigued him at the time. He inevitably started by joking about his little solo firm and his lack of interest in the business of law.

But his intellectual conviction would eventually overcome his ironic self-awareness, and his fervor for his latest cause would ignite his verbal energy. Then he would leap up on stage as if someone had pulled the strings on his marionette body, launching an argument astonishing in its complexity, insight, and elegance. It was unlike any practice of law she had imagined.

And he was unlike any man she had known. He never lectured from notes. Often she suspected that he was fabricating at least some of the tales he related in class. But she discovered that each story had some basis in reality, though often slanted to enhance the entertainment over the educational value. A lobster really did have ten thousand eyes and saw by reflection rather than refraction. The Hawaiian name of the endangered monk seal was Ilio holo I ka uaua, which really did mean "the dog that goes in rough water." And the Minnesota Department of Natural Resources did in fact sponsor a volunteer loon survey, though it was not, as he suggested, a survey of volunteer loons. Nor was the questionnaire he handed out to the class ever approved by the state.

Once he told the story of Henry David Thoreau and Mosquito Pie.

"On a journey to Minnesota in 1861," he said, "the famous author and naturalist Henry David Thoreau visited Minneapolis and cataloged many unknown species of Minnesota wildlife. Of these, the most famous by far was the St. Anthony mosquito, which, he reported in letters, was the size of a common wren.

"Early Minneapolitans hunted mosquitoes in the marshes, and mosquito pie had long been considered a local delicacy. Based on Thoreau's enthusiastic report, the pie was soon shipped worldwide, becoming as popular as beaver hats and buffalo robes in some European circles.

"In 1911 the city of Minneapolis finally dredged the marshes to encourage settlement in the area. Canals were built to allow boat passage among the lakes. And the series of parks now known as the Grand Round of Minneapolis took its modern shape.

"The loss of the wetlands, however, along with extensive overhunting to supply the relentless European demand, contributed to the extinction of the St. Anthony mosquito. And mosquito pie vanished forever from American frontier cuisine."

She was certain this time that she had detected a fabrication. But when she researched the story, she found that Thoreau had in fact traveled to Minneapolis in 1861 in the hope that the dry plains air would cure his consumption. She could never confirm or deny the part about mosquito pie, though she had seen (and felt) large enough mosquitoes in Minnesota to lend some credence to the possibility.

To deal with the unpredictable array of his lecture topics, she established an intricate and precise organizational scheme for her notes. Each subject area was tabbed with a particular color. Animal rights was red. Air quality was blue. Water quality was green. Wildlife regulation was yellow. Miscellaneous was purple.

During class, she found herself leafing back and forth among colors as his lecture topics ranged from the mating habits of the endangered Queen Alexandra Birdwing butterfly to the effect of automobile emissions on sunsets. As the semester progressed, the lecture topics began to rotate in errant patterns that sent her flipping through her notebook pages in an unremitting determination to categorize.

One day toward the end of the term, as she was frantically juggling colors to track the bizarre minutiae of his legal scholarship, she flipped too hard and her notebook spun noisily across the lecture room floor.

Everything stopped.

She looked up.

Everyone was watching her.

She turned to him to apologize and saw the enormous grin he was incapable of hiding. Suddenly the maddening vectors of lecture topics throughout the term fell into place for her. He had done it for her. Or to her. She arched her brow and asked: "Professor. My notebook. Would you mind?"

After class, he asked her out for coffee. After coffee, he asked to take her home.

"You had this all planned," she said.

"I don't make plans," he answered. "I have Visions."

Those words slipped inside her like a key into a lock.

"What vision do you have for us?" she asked.

He closed his eyes, conjured the answer.

"For the rest of your life, you'll never doubt that no one could love you like I do."

She wrestled with the double negative.

"Is that a good thought or a bad thought?" she asked finally.

"Yes," he said. Then he kissed her.

Her eyes opened as the key turned.

He was better at Saturday afternoons than anyone she had ever known. A trip to the grocery store was an adventure. A matinee was a vacation. But staying home was paradise.

The purple-and-black graduation gown rustled in the wind outside Northrop Memorial Auditorium while the tassel dangling from the mortarboard cap swung annoyingly from side to side in front of her eyes.

"I look like a raisin with a flat head," she said.

"You do not," he said. "Raisins don't have heads."

She flipped the tassel to one side and smoothed out the ruffling folds.

"You are always such a comfort."

"I try," he said, rearranging the mortarboard.

"Don't. Leave. Not the hair."

He backed away.

"Thank you," she said, pulling out a mirror and checking the damage. "I have got to find a new brand of hairspray."

He took her hands.

"You look stunning," he said. "Don't worry. You've been through this before. And I promise not to whistle from the faculty seating area."

She glared.

"Don't even . . ."

"I promised."

In the short time they had been together, she had come to learn that that word meant something to him. He seldom used it. And he never said it when he didn't mean it.

It was not exactly a guarantee, despite the best of his intentions, especially if it involved dry cleaning, a process he found both environmentally unsustainable and socially unnecessary. Though he made an exception for his signature blue suits. For someone with a prodigious, even legendary, memory for legal arcana, he had very little hold on the details of everyday life. She finally decided it had to do with his attention—not the span of it, but the extraordinary force of it.

A promise *not* to do something was more reliable, though, and he had promised not to embarrass her. She was fairly certain he would not whistle. But she would not have been surprised at a serenade.

"Be good," she said. "This is important to me. These are my future colleagues."

A look passed over his face, one she had seen once or twice before. She had thought about that look and deduced that somehow his imagination leapt over or into or through uncounted alternate futures and somehow coalesced into a vision. It was a vision he would not, possibly could not express. But it was a future shared. She was sure of that. The thrill made her shiver. He wrapped his arms around her.

"I am so proud of you," he said.

She rested her head against his shoulder. She no longer cared whether anyone saw them together. For several months, at her request, they had carefully hidden the fact that they were seeing one another, were all but living together in his Warehouse District loft. But there was no longer any need or desire for privacy on her part. He had never cared.

"I'd better go in," she said, pushing away.

The graduation ceremony lasted an hour and forty-five minutes. The guest speaker was a former university law school graduate and current associate justice on the Minnesota Supreme Court who spoke eloquently on the responsibilities of the advocate in modern society and signed autographs after the ceremony.

Standing backstage afterward, she joked and shared congratulations with a few others among the graduating class, comparing notes on various professors and answering pointed questions about one in particular.

He rushed up to her, carrying a large package wrapped in brown paper.

"We have to go," he announced.

"What is it?" she asked.

He grabbed her hand.

"It's an emergency."

"What about the reception?" she asked, running along with him as quickly as she could in the long, encumbering gown. The cap fell somewhere behind her. "This is a rental. I have to pay for that."

"Here," he said, stopping suddenly and reaching for the zipper. "Get that thing off."

She slapped his hand away instinctively.

He laughed.

"What are you wearing under there?" he asked.

"Not enough," she answered. "I thought it might be hot in the auditorium."

"Good thinking," he answered, smiling. "Here. Put this on."

He handed her the package. The return address said Italy; she did not recognize the name of the town. She opened the wrapping paper carefully, not fully trusting his taste in graduation presents.

Inside the package was a suit, a dark burgundy silk with an almost invisible pinstripe that complemented the hue of his perpetually favorite costume.

"Try it on," he said.

She slipped into the ladies' room and changed. The fit was impossibly perfect. She had never seen such exquisite tailoring, certainly could never have afforded it herself. In the mirror, her long slender limbs and willowy frame, which she had often imagined gangly and ungraceful, now seemed dynamic, even daunting, as if she absorbed powers from the outfit itself. All she needed, she mused, was a cape.

He nodded as she emerged.

"Stunning."

"So where are you taking me?"

"Someplace you have wanted to go for years."

"Italy?"

"Better. Court."

Hand in hand, they left the building, descended two at a time the broad steps outside, and entered the waiting limo, his preferred method of transportation if he could not walk. She preferred the bicycle. Neither of them liked to drive. She had no idea how he could afford to travel by limousine, since his small practice never seemed to bring in any money that she was aware of. And neither his speaking fees nor his university salary were likely to add up to much.

As the limo pulled away, she turned to him.

"You have a court date today?"

"Yes," he answered. "The most important case I've ever had."

"You haven't mentioned it before."

"You've been busy with finals and graduation."

"So what am I doing here? You need an audience?"

He took her hand.

"I need your help."

She was puzzled.

"Since when do you need my help?"

The limo turned the corner onto Hennepin Avenue and sped past the lofty downtown buildings.

"I need you to be my co-counsel."

She was even more puzzled.

"I haven't passed the bar. I don't have a license. If anyone found out—"

"Would I let you risk everything? I just need it to look like my firm is more than a one-person shop."

She shook her head.

"It will be fine. I promise," he whispered.

"I have a bad feeling about this."

"Trust me."

The limo pulled up outside the county courtroom. She stepped out. The brilliant sunshine blinded her for a moment.

"So what is this case about?" she asked as they headed for the courtroom.

"Oh, don't worry about that. Just scowl at the other side once in a while."

"I'll pretend it's you."

He pushed through the double doors of the courtroom. She hesitated behind him, pausing a moment out of respect. In the few months they had been together, she had adopted his almost spiritual apprehension of The Law as a great imaginative human force for balance and justice. The Law as taught, The Law as intended— not the law as practiced.

The courtroom was small and almost empty. The judge was sitting behind the bench. Another man waited at a table on the left. A third man was already seated at the witness stand. Yet they were all connected, and beholden to, that greater numinous entity.

Despite her anxiety, she felt both exhilarated and confident. She knew that whatever happened in this room, she could handle it.

"You're late," the judge admonished them.

"Sorry, Your Honor. Our previous engagement ran long," he replied.

"I'd say this one was a little more important, wouldn't you?"

"Yes, Your Honor. We apologize."

"Great," she whispered as they passed through the vacant gallery and sat side by side at the empty table. "I have no license and we've already antagonized the judge."

He squeezed her hand.

"Don't worry so much."

He stood.

"Your Honor, I call the defendant to the stand."

He moved around behind her. His large right hand rested on her shoulder. Underneath the stiff fall of her hair, his thumb traced the line of her neck. He bent down to whisper in her ear.

"Watch this."

She twisted in her seat to glance up at him, then turned back quickly to watch.

He stepped out from behind the table.

She pulled over the folder on the table and began to examine the stack of papers inside for some clue as to what was going on. The papers were blank, except for row after row after row of little hearts with arrows through them.

She stood immediately.

"Your Honor," she said, "it's getting late in the day. I suggest we reconvene until tomorrow."

"It's one-thirty. We just finished lunch," the judge replied.

"Right. Sorry, Your Honor," she said.

The judge turned back to him.

"Continue."

He glanced at her, pleading silently for some clue.

"Your Honor," he said finally, "may I have a minute to confer with my co-counsel?"

"Make it fast," said the judge.

She stood quickly. He descended to one knee.

"I imagine that I will love you for as long as we both shall live."

"What are you—"

He brought her face down to his, kissing her. She thought she was pulling away but found after a few seconds that she wasn't.

"Thank you, Your Honor," he said finally. "I believe we are ready to continue."

He vaulted over the table, spilling the paper hearts all over the floor.

The judge gaveled furiously.

"Counselor!"

He turned to the judge, surprised.

"Yes, Your Honor?"

The judge glared and pointed his finger.

"I want to see counsel at the bench. Immediately!"

He stepped forward, along with the other attorney. Even the witness leaned in from the stand.

The judge aimed the gavel at her.

"That means you too, young lady."

She rose and approached, marshaling her courage. The judge glared.

"Where is your license?" the judge asked.

"Your Honor," she started, "I'm here simply as—"

"I have it!" he interrupted, removing a crumpled document from deep within the breast pocket of his suit. He unfolded and smoothed it before handing it to the judge too quickly for her to see. It looked official but she couldn't tell what it said.

The judge inspected the document carefully, then examined her over his wire-rimmed glasses.

"Very well. This seems to be in order," he grunted and then handed the paper to her.

She looked at it carefully, but could not process the information for a second, as if it were written in a language she could not translate.

It was not a license to practice law.

It was a marriage license.

Now the judge was smiling.

As was the other attorney.

And the witness.

In moving to the Midwest, she had secretly hoped she would encounter a cyclone. But she had never imagined one would take up permanent residence in her life.

She looked over at him, standing two feet away, not smiling but somehow embodying a smile. His eyes burned with that vision. And then she had a vision of her own, not of her life (though she sensed, had always sensed, that her life would be joyful but not happy) but of him, the true him, the him she could not possibly yet know but nevertheless for this one moment had access to.

And with that vision came a sign that the choice she must make had already been made, and that he knew it already, had known it, and that it was the same for him. The elemental forces had aligned. A word of resistance would alter their course. But no resistance was possible or even at that moment conceivable for either of them. He slipped a ring on her finger.

The judge began.

"Will you take this man to be your husband?"

And then she saw.

There was no bailiff.

No clerk.

No court reporter.

No gallery.

No trial.

Just a judge.

And two witnesses, not one.

She turned to him.

"In a courtroom?"

"Where else should two attorneys get married?"

The uncut ruby welled over her finger like blood. But the color matched her suit perfectly.

"I do," she said.

"Me too," he added.

The librarian glared at both of them as he descended to one knee. Her face sank out of sight behind a volume of the Minnesota Statutes Supplement.

"Please?" he begged.

"No," she whispered.

He shifted to the other knee.

"Please?"

"No. Be quiet."

Both knees.

"Please?"

"No."

"I want you. Only you. Forever," he declared.

"I believe you. No."

She decided to move for summary judgment.

"I love you," she continued, "in a way I never knew was possible. I am happily married to you. I love our life. I love our time together. So please don't misunderstand when I tell you that the thought of spending every day twenty-four hours a day with you is absolutely appalling."

He got up off his knees.

"I'm a brilliant lawyer," he said. "Brilliant lawyers win clients. But great lawyers win cases. You're a great lawyer. Or you will be. I know it."

"So you're saying I'm not brilliant?"

"No. Of course you're brilliant. Just. Not relatively. But. You know. Vice versa."

"Did you ask me to marry you so I would join your firm? Because that would be . . ."

"Absolutely not!"

"Flattering—"

"Really?"

"In a deeply disturbing way."

He took her hand.

"Look," he said, "this is the thing. Separately we can do good things. Together we can do great things. We have an obligation to our own wonderfulness."

"Save the whales?" she asked.

"I know some very nice whales."

"Save the rainforest?"

"It's the least we can do."

She took back her hand.

"Who's going to save us?" she asked.

"Every relationship requires some sacrifice."

"Not usually human."

"Okay," she said at last, discovering she could laugh and shudder at the same time. "Partners. But let me pass the bar first please. Okay?"

"Okay."

The librarian wagged her finger, warning them both.

It was her third time accompanying him. Every year he flew into Florence, drove narrow roads rising through orchards and falling through vineyards to the tiny village of Collodi, where he bought five blue suits of the same superfine wool cloth, each handmade by Maestro Carlo. At the end of the day, they would have tea at the stunning seventeenth-century gardens of the Villa Garzoni, then inevitably spend an hour or two at the Parco di Pinocchio, the exquisitely designed park commemorating the adventures of the famous puppet.

She knew the small hill town well, the constricted cobblestone passage, you couldn't call it a street, ascending the mountain past immaculate terra-cotta homes. But after several hours of wandering, she finally decided she was lost, and did not care. The town was perfect: espresso served in tiny cups older than any place she'd ever been; alleys so narrow and winding you could walk for hours and be home in minutes; rainbow food in rainbow bowls under roofs that had sheltered Medicis; wine fresh as morning.

Finally, turning a corner, she peered through the afternoon glare on a shop window to find the puppet perched in the window box, the familiar gray-and-white face gazing contentedly out over the Piazza del Piccolo, keeping a watchful button eye out for straying Italian sheep (unruly but well groomed). She stooped to enter, bracing herself on the worn lintel until her eyes adjusted to the relative dark.

"Perfecto," said the maestro.

"He's not talking about the suit," he said.

She smiled at him. He descended from the tailor's block and glided toward her, one sleeve on, one sleeve off.

"Here," he said. "Tonight."

"We'll see," she answered.

Every day when she came home, she found Sancho somewhere new. Washing the dishes. Vacuuming the oriental carpets. Hiding in a closet (inside her raincoat). Sliding down the banister. Reading to the other stuffed animals (of which there were many). Once he even greeted her at the door sitting on top of the coat rack with roses scrunched between his padded white paws.

Soon the variations became more frequent. When she left the room, he might be on the sofa. When she came back, he would be rocking in the rocking chair. Or he would have changed the channel on the television. Or taken a bite from her candy bar.

No one else was ever around.

When the possibilities at home were exhausted, she began discovering him at the office. Hiding in a file cabinet. Sitting in her chair. Writing a letter to Santa Paws on her computer. Perusing her law books with tiny bifocals perched on his furry white muzzle.

It was the most charming coercion she had ever experienced.

The crystal surface of the desk glittered silver in the moonlight shining through the office windows. Six months before, they had finally moved out of his cramped yet colorful loft space in the Warehouse District and into the more professional setting in the Wells Fargo Building, which she had carefully designed and furnished.

He was a dark outline against the night. She was grateful that she could not see his face.

"I'm sorry. I have to," she said almost to herself.

"Okay."

"I'll buy out your share of the house."

"Okay."

"And the firm. I know you started it but—"

"Okay."

"I'll have someone we know draw up the papers."

"Okay."

"It's for the best."

Somehow she felt him smile.

"I don't want the best," he said. "I want you."

A litany played through her mind of every hope fulfilled and left dangling in the failure of the wrong success.

"You make me laugh," she said.

"Okay," he replied. "Okay."

CHAPTER 4

An Ever-Fixed Mark

Like the New Jerusalem of the Book of Revelation, the modern city of Minneapolis lies foursquare, split into quadrants by Highways 94 and 35. The heart of the city is the Mississippi River, which flows through the center before wending east and south all the way to the Gulf of Mexico.

Hennepin Island stands in the river at very nearly the center of Minneapolis, just upstream from the University of Minnesota, just downstream from the old Pillsbury flour mill and St. Anthony Falls. The falls were "discovered" by Father Louis Hennepin, a missionary and historian who traveled with La Salle in 1678 on his first expedition to La Nouvelle France. He named the falls after his favorite saint, the patron of monks and hermits. Father Hennepin had a history of making history with waterfalls, having been the first European to write home about Niagara.

In the middle of the nineteenth century, a four-story building was constructed near the northern end of Hennepin Island. Initially the structure housed either a boardinghouse or a bordello (no one is certain which, or perhaps it was both) serving the nearby mills. But in the 1880s, the St. Anthony Inn opened at the site. Renowned for its Gilded Age furnishings and the first electric chandeliers in Minnesota, the inn catered to visiting royalty, ex-presidents like Rutherford B. Hayes, and touring celebrities such as Mark Twain.

The inn closed finally during the Great Depression. Empty during the war years, the building was donated to the city in 1955. For forty-some years, the Minneapolis city administration stored excess furniture and office supplies within the neglected historic walls.

About a year after they were married, Nick and Lena spotted the dilapidated structure on one of their long bike rides down the river-bank through the St. Anthony area. They bought the building from the city after a series of successful cases put their tiny law firm in solid financial territory. Like many other affluent couples, they briefly flirted with the idea of opening a bed and breakfast at the site, restoring the name of the St. Anthony Inn. But the realities of their flourishing practice made that idea unworkable, for which Lena at least was truly grateful. She and Nick eventually renovated the top floor and lived there during the last year of their marriage.

After the divorce, Lena leased the first floor of the building to a restaurant. The second floor consisted of offices, mostly unused. The third floor was converted into condos. Lena lived alone in a suite on the remodeled fourth floor.

Harvey Larson worked for Lena as building manager, handy-man, sometime private investigator, and occasional Nick wrangler. A burly ex-marine, he lived rent-free on the third floor, which gave Lena a sense of extra security; though the island was in the middle of the city, it felt dark and isolated at night. Harvey was also very good at tracking Nick down when necessary, which was often enough in the years following the divorce that he and Nick had become good friends.

As Lena and Nick approached, Harvey held open the door to the lobby, nodding a smile to Lena and tilting a questioning look at Nick as he passed by. Nick put a finger to his lips. Harvey nodded and gave Nick a subtle thumbs-up.

Under Lena's meticulous direction, the lobby had been restored to gilded elegance using early-twentieth-century photographs of the St. Anthony Inn. She had installed the elevator only after extensive (and expensive) negotiations with the St. Anthony Historic Preservation League. The glittering silver doors of the elevator were matched by ornate antique mirrors on the opposite wall. Nick and Lena surrogates waited for the elevator in infinite regression. Lena's doppelgängers smiled to excess.

"Doesn't this violate the divorce decree?" Nick asked.

"Yes," said Lena, still smiling.

"So basically you could have me shot at any time?"

"Yes," said Lena, still smiling.

For the first time since the divorce, Nick and Lena walked together over the uneven hardwood bands of the fourth-floor corridor. Lena entered the apartment, leaving the door open. Nick hesitated.

Lena looked back.

"You coming in?"

"I never thought you'd ask me that again."

"Don't touch anything."

"Now, that sounds like you."

Nick took a few steps into the large foyer and halted, reexamining the space.

"You've changed things."

"For the better."

Nick drifted into the living room.

"You've changed the lighting," he said.

"And."

"You bought a new rug."

"And."

One after another, Nick enumerated each piece of furniture. Then he laughed.

"You got rid of every piece of furniture we ever had sex on."

"Except one," Lena replied.

"Which one?"

"Well, I guess technically the washing machine isn't furniture."

Nick nodded.

"We'll always have spin cycle."

In the living room, Lena checked her messages. Preston's voice filtered through the room: "What are you thinking of, letting him back into your life? Do you know the definition of insanity? Call me. Maybe I can get you out of it."

Lena looked at Nick. "Wait right there," she said finally.

She left the living room and headed down the hallway. Nick sampled the chair that had replaced his recliner, setting Sancho on the back and sinking into the plush. Lena charged back into the living room with a stack of music CDs. Nick struggled to get to his feet.

"I've been meaning to give these to you," she said.

From across the room, she sailed a CD at Nick like a knife-edged Frisbee.

"Hey—"

She flipped another. Nick dodged.

"Wait—"

Another. Nick jumped.

"What—"

Nick held up his hands. Lena paused.

"Tell me," she said.

Lena launched one more, which soared over Nick's head and bounced off the mantel over the fireplace. He picked it up and examined it carefully.

"You broke Nat King Cole."

"Tell me why," she insisted as she zipped one more at him. He caught this one and held it up for her.

"And David Bowie is cracked."

She held up the next one for him. He saw the label and pointed.

"No! Not that one," he pleaded.

Lena brandished the CD like a martial-arts weapon.

"Tell me why," she demanded, "or John Philip Sousa is a casualty of war."

"Why what?"

"You knew the judge would order supervision. And you knew I would agree. Now what I want to know is why?"

"Lena, I had no idea the judge would do that."

Lena tested the wind factor and started winding up for the launch.

"Wait!" Nick shouted, then softly, avoiding her eyes: "This is hard."

Lena waited. Nick finally looked up.

"I don't think I can get through this alone."

Lena removed the CD from the plastic case and pressed the disk between her palms.

"I mean it!" she warned.

Nick smiled and shrugged.

"Okay, okay. You want to know why?"

Lena paused, then nodded.

"You still feel guilty about the divorce," Nick explained. "I'm giving you one last chance to make it up to me."

Lena was speechless for only a moment.

"That is absolutely ridiculous! I have nothing to feel guilty about."

Nick settled himself back in the new chair.

"I know that," he replied. "But *you* don't."

Lena stomped over to Nick, poised to either argue or attack, then dropped the CD into his lap. Nick pulled his long legs up into lotus position and spread his hands wide.

"If it's not guilt," he asked, "then why?"

Lena started to respond, then stopped.

She started again.

And stopped again.

Finally she said: "Work. Go. I have to. Here. Stay. Do not leave."

She grabbed her keys and purse and left quickly. Nick bounced mildly, testing the overstuffed chair. He held Sancho up.

"Who do you love?" he asked.

Dark eyes glimmered with recessed illumination.

Lena strode back and forth in front of her desk conversing with the air. The telephone headset swung perilously at each sudden period.

"But there must be. I know that but. This is a condition of. Yes. Please. Could you hold, please?"

After Nick left the firm, Lena was overwhelmed. But it was not the caseload that made her distraught; she welcomed the opportunity to focus on something other than her personal life. And it was not the duties of running a successful law firm; she had far more business acumen (and far more interest in the financial aspects) than Nick had ever had, and she had been running the firm, more or less, for some time.

It was not even being alone that had bothered her, as such. With Nick gone, Lena was overwhelmed by the silence. Nick was never quiet. Even on the few occasions when he wasn't talking, he was always buzzing about the office, humming, reciting poetry, singing, rustling papers, shuffling books, bustling around in an urgent search for the books and papers he had just rustled and shuffled.

After he left, the lack of noise in the office was nerve-racking. Any sound but the ringing of the telephone was welcome. Lena invited clients in without cause and took them to lunch more than necessary. She spent more time reorganizing than reading, because the shuffling noise was many times more satisfying than the occasional turn of a page.

Sharon, a refugee from the Midwest comedy-club circuit by way of Twin Cities Temps, had been her sardonic salvation. Several years before, Sharon had left unfinished her biography of Laurence Sterne and tried her luck as a stand-up comedian. Life on the gritty road of comedy and even grittier one-night stands finally wore her down, so she took a break, bought a condo in the Uptown area of Minneapolis, and applied for work through the temp agency.

Ward and Grant was her first and only position. After a week, Lena hired her outright as office manager, grateful for both her wit and her editorial skills. Sharon speculated that they had been friends for a thousand lifetimes. Privately Lena suspected something of the same sort.

Sitting outside Lena's office, Sharon was now thoroughly engaged in *Anna Karenina*. On the opposite wall, she noted the appearance of a shadow, vaguely human in form, with a disheveled halo. The shadow gestured dramatically.

Lena balanced on one leg while poking her head out the door of her office, *en point au décolletage*. The halo wobbled in concert with a circlet of hair sticking up through the metal band of her headset.

"Get my house on the phone, please," Lena requested.

"You must have one of those smart houses," Sharon noted.

"No. I mean, call my house."

"I'm pretty sure you're already here."

"No. Look. There's a man at my house."

"About time."

"Not that kind of man."

"Is there another kind?"

"It's Nick."

Sharon grabbed for the phone.

"Should I call an ambulance? Fire department? SWAT team?"

Lena closed her eyes.

"Just. Get him on the phone."

Sharon nodded. Lena pirouetted back to her desk and took the caller off hold.

"Hello? Look, anything will—what? An animal shelter is perfect. He loves animals. These are live animals, right? Could you hold on, please?"

Lena switched calls.

"Nick? Oh, hello, Dr. Richardson. You can? Wonderful. When? He'll be there. Thank you."

She switched back.

"Hello? When should he? He'll be there. Oh. One thing. There's a puppet. P-u-p-p-e-t. That's a good question. If you find out, let me know. Thanks."

She hung up and slumped into her chair.

"I'm the one who needs a psychiatric exam."

Sharon entered *glissade,* her headset securely ensconced.

"No answer. I'm getting your—"

Frantically, Lena gestured to Sharon.

"Hang up the phone. Hang up the phone. Don't get the—"

"Want to leave a message?"

The phone in Lena's living room was ringing. Nick looked over but didn't move. A deep voice emerged from the TV: "Today is E day.

"E is for Exciting.

"E is for Excellent.

"E is for Electricity."

A cartoon figure stuck a finger in a light socket and lit up. Nick chuckled.

The voice switched to the answering machine, but it was Nick's own voice. Nick Then said to Nick Now: "Hi, Nick and Lena can't come to the phone right now, so leave a message and we'll call you back in three point four minutes."

There was laughter, then a beep, then silence. Nick covered Sancho's ears.

Lena struggled into the apartment, managing the heavy door while carrying mail, keys, briefcase, and a grocery bag.

Nick cradled Sancho in the chair, legs dangling over legs dangling over the arm, enrapt in a Charlie Brown special—*A Midsummer Night's Peanuts,* with Snoopy in the role of Puck.

"Little help, please?" Lena asked.

"Sure."

The puppet came flying directly at Lena. She dropped mail, briefcase, and grocery bag, spilling all three over the floor of the foyer. She held on to the keys. And she caught Sancho.

"Thanks," Lena muttered.

Nick got up and walked over to Lena, examining the debris.

"You weren't much help," he complained to Sancho.

He kissed Lena on the cheek, gathered the groceries, and smiled.

"Nice message on the answering machine," he said.

Arms full, Nick headed for the kitchen.

"Just. Shut up," Lena called after him.

Nick, heading back out of the kitchen, shook his head.

"We never talk anymore."

He looked at Lena, silent for a moment.

"Whatever happened to us?" he asked.

Lena estimated the distance, judged the trajectory, charged forward for about ten feet, then launched herself into Nick, knocking him down and sitting on him.

"Oh yeah, now I remember," Nick said.

Lena shifted her center of gravity off Nick's solar plexus, against the solidity of the wall.

"You exhaust me," she sighed.

Nick moved next to her, and her head tilted down against his shoulder.

"Sorry," he whispered eventually. Lena didn't say anything, but settled in deeper. He waited a few moments before speaking again.

"Guest room, I assume," he said.

"You know what they say about assumptions."

"What?"

"Sometimes they are absolutely right."

Nick slowly straightened, stood, and stretched his back and neck, which cracked and creaked audibly. Then he reached down to help Lena up. He held her hand in both of his for a second, then traveled slowly down the hall toward the guest room.

The hallway was unlit. As he piloted his way along the wall, his fingertips skipped automatically over the pictures hanging below his eye level. In the dark, the content of the photos was not visible. At one time, the frames had held photos of trips they had taken together, mixing business with pleasure at speaking engagements all around the world. Nick had been highly sought after as a speaker on environmental legislation, and Lena had begun to develop a reputation of her own on legal issues related to international human rights.

At the door to the guest room, Nick's fingers drifted down to the antique door handle rescued from a dustbin in the basement. Before entering, he announced loudly to Lena's silhouette, framed softly in the incandescent foyer: "I just want you to know I'm locking my door tonight."

He disappeared into the room. The door clicked shut.

Lena also moved with assurance down the darkened hall. At the door, she whispered: "Nick?"

"Yes?"

"I just want you to know."

"Yes?"

"I'm locking your door too."

Lena chunked tight the padlock Harvey had installed on the door, then walked back into the light. Nick heard her whistling her way down the hall. An eyebrow raised to meet the challenge.

Lena woke to dark eyes staring down at her. Sancho leaned against the lamp on her nightstand, holding a crimson rose.

She sighed, then explained to Sancho: "It's not you."

She picked the puppet up and held him for a moment. Then she placed him on the bed, put on her pink silk robe, dumped the rose in the trash, and walked out of the bedroom.

Nick's door was still closed and padlocked. She dialed the combination, slipped the padlock out of the ring, enclosed it in her fist, and knocked. The guest room door toppled inward off its hinges like a stop-action colossus. Closing her mouth, she moved back up the hall.

The kitchen was nearly as large as the living room. The original stone fireplace, tall enough to stand in, contrasted with the recently acquired stainless-steel appliances at the other end. Whenever she lit a fire (which was not often), the reflection transformed the kitchen into a brushed scarlet inferno.

A wood-block island in the middle of the kitchen bridged the eras. Nick sat on a stool by the island, doing the crossword, stirring his coffee with a hinge pin. Lena shuffled in wordlessly, sat across from him, grabbed the paper, and examined his answers.

"These are all wrong."

"In what way?"

"In the way of not being right."

"They fit."

Lena looked closely. The words did fit in the spaces. And they did fit with each other. But they had nothing to do with the clues.

"They give you clues so that you can get the answers. They don't give them so you can at all costs avoid the right word."

"That's what they'd like you to believe," Nick said, taking the paper back.

"It's my crossword. Don't abuse it."

"Fine," he said and continued his work, entering the correct answers this time, though upside down and backward.

"Coffee?"

He poured her a cup from a pewter decanter she didn't know she owned. She took a sip.

"Look. This isn't going to work unless—"

She took another sip.

"This is good coffee," she continued.

Nick inhaled the arousing perfume of the brew he'd bought at Sebastian Joe's a half hour earlier.

"Thanks," he said.

Then Lena slammed down the coffee mug.

"Damn you, Nick," she complained. "You are *not* going to turn me into a commercial."

"I'm sensing that something is wrong."

He looked up from his crossword. Lena's long hair was free and tangled and her slightly bloodshot eyes crinkled as she squinted against the morning. Her robe slipped open, revealing rumpled blush pajamas, whose three unbuttoned buttons briefly took his breath.

"Look," said Lena, pulling her robe closed. "This is not going to work unless you stop this."

"Stop making coffee?"

"Yes. No. Yes. Stop trying to do whatever you're trying to do. Whatever that is. Not that I ever understand what it is."

"I'm just trying to show my appreciation."

"Stop it!"

"What?"

"Being nice to me. It creeps me out."

Nick smiled.

"I could send roses. . . ."

Lena stood, managing to stamp both feet at once.

"No roses! I mean it, Nick."

Lena began circumnavigating the island, round and round, as she spoke. Nick swiveled on his stool to track her progress.

"Look," said Lena north by northwest.

Then "Look," west by southwest.

Then "Look," east by southeast. "You'll be here until you complete your community service, which should be around four weeks. So the only way this is going to work is if we have as little contact as possible. So. So. So I'm going to get ready for work and then I will drive you to the animal shelter."

She stopped. Nick continued to spin on the stool until she grabbed his shoulders, and then composed herself.

"Now," she said. "I'm going back to the bedroom."

Nick started to rise. Lena interjected her hand palm up.

"Stay."

Nick stayed and sipped his coffee.

"Now, that's good coffee," he noted and smiled like the Mona Lisa.

Lena massaged the shampoo into her hair with one hand while holding her cell phone out of the shower with the other. She yelled beyond the hazy glass divide into the blooming fog of steam.

"Hi. I got your message but I can't talk about it now. Everything is arranged. He's seeing Dr. Richardson and volunteering at the animal shelter. What? Yes, the animal shelter. It's not that funny. Okay, it is that funny. Thanks for yesterday. It meant a lot. I'll call you later."

Bubbles slithered down Lena's body while an avalanche of suds dangled over her brow. She closed her eyes and slipped her face under the torrent of the shower. The water enfolded her, descending into a milky whirlpool at her feet.

Lena groped out with her other soapy hand, punched "End," and dialed another number.

"It's me. I'll be in soon. Call the phone company and tell them I want a waterproof speakerphone installed in my shower. My shower. No, I'm not starting a 900 number."

She hung up, then lifted onto her toes and reached toward the sink. Her torso inclined against the flimsy rigidity of the glass shower door as her hand sought desperately for somewhere dry, when a furry paw slipped the phone from her grasp.

"Get out of here, Nick," Lena warned. "I mean it. Or when you get to the animal shelter I'm having you neutered."

Lena turned off the shower and listened. No sound. She tiptoed over the chilly tile and checked the door. Closed. She looked back. As the steam parted, she saw Sancho on the sink next to her phone, bath cap on his head, washcloth strategically placed, from which emerged the crimson rose.

Lena smiled and sighed.

"It's still not you."

Lena's car passed through the broken chain-link gate and stopped at the top of the circular driveway. A single green metal door was the only apparent entrance to the massive two-story cinder-block fortress that constituted the Hennepin Animal Shelter. An asphalt courtyard marked with yellow stripes lay between the surrounding barbed-wire fence and the dirty walls.

"I take it the word 'shelter' is a euphemism," Nick muttered.

As he opened the car door, Lena put a hand on his arm.

"I think you should leave Sancho with me."

"You're right," Nick agreed. "This is no place for him."

He handed the puppet to Lena and got out of the car. The Porsche sped away before he could change his mind.

At the door, Nick hesitated but finally stepped inside. A short passageway opened into a wide rectangular reception area. On

the walls, deteriorating corkboards displayed faded legal announce-
ments, regulations regarding every conceivable aspect of shelter
operation.

A woman sat behind a desk in the lobby, so short that her bright
saffron blouse was almost entirely concealed by the clutter on the
desk. The nameplate read:

ALICE WILSON, PH.D.
DIRECTOR, HENNEPIN ANIMAL SHELTER

Nick approached slowly.

"My name is Nick Ward," he said.

She didn't look up.

"There's a chalk line in front of the desk," she said. "If you
can tell me what it means, we can use you. If not, good luck somewhere else."

Nick looked down. Beneath his feet, a straight line was drawn in
yellow chalk.

"It means a very thin person was killed here recently."

Alice didn't respond.

"It means you're the queen bee and I'm the worker bee."

Alice still didn't respond.

"It means this is where the desk goes."

Alice wrenched her eyes up from the papers covering the desk.
She examined Nick silently for a long time. Then she looked back
down and said: "Go on in."

Nick's eyes narrowed.

"I was right?"

Alice didn't look up.

"You were right the first time."

She pointed down the hall. Nick backed slowly away from the desk and continued down the passageway.

"Scary," he whispered, shaking his head.

"I heard that," echoed behind him.

He hurried down the corridor, passing several empty offices and finally reaching a double-bolted door. He pulled it open and froze in place.

The room was cavernous, a warehouse-sized abyss, dim in spite of long racks of dusty fluorescent lights suspended above. Spidery thin girders braced the high ceiling. Beneath the iron web, steel cages extended into the distance, row after row a football field long. Dozens of them. Maybe hundreds. From where Nick stood, no animals were visible. But howls and yelps echoed through the cinder and steel wasteland.

On a table by the door, Nick discovered a wine crate. Inside a litter of kittens slept amid the din, tiny chests of black and white fluttering in an intricate confusion of shifting paws and twisting tails.

Nick proceeded down the center aisle, wandering slowly between the steel enclosures, observing right then left. There were a few unoccupied cages, but even those gave evidence of recent habitation. A blanket. A dish. A chewed-up toy. But most of the cages were occupied. Each inhabitant (all canine) was identified with a white three-by-five card taped to the door of the cell.

3224 Bloodhound mix male.

3226 Spaniel male neutered.

3227 Alsatian female.

3228 Beagle male puppy.

3231 Sheepdog/husky mix male.

3232 Shepherd mix female spayed.

3233 Schnauzer mix female.

3234 Labrador retriever mix male neutered.

3211 Wolfhound male.

3211 lifted his shaggy head. Great eyes flashed in the vibrating light as he began to stand, slowly unwinding from front to back until his enormous muzzle was even with Nick's chest. The dog unwound further, lifting his paws against the steel cage front until Nick looked directly into the huge eyes, black in the slash of sunlight that poured through the high window. The dirty beam of light fell to Nick's feet, spotlighting the dusty slab on which he stood, highlighting the great beast's profile.

Nick took out a pen, scratched out "3211," and wrote: "Wolfram."

"Now I know why I was sent here," Nick said.

The dog's pink ears pricked up.

"Then you're doing better than I am," a great penumbrous voice responded.

Nick spun around. The tall man before him wore a dark-green uniform with "Ralph" emblazoned on the left breast. His hair was cropped, and he wore thick leather work gloves that might once have been green also. Nick held out his hand and said: "Nick."

Ralph put a leash in Nick's extended hand and said: "Ralph."

Nick looked curiously at the leash.

"Am I supposed to wear this?"

Ralph didn't smile but finally said: "They told me you were funny."

"Who is that really scary woman out front?"

"That's Alice. She's my wife."

Nick started to laugh. But Ralph wasn't joking.

"I liked her immediately." Nick nodded.

Ralph and Alice had met at a party twenty-three years earlier. Alice was studying management science and statistics at the University of Alabama. Ralph was in a master's program in wildlife conservation at Auburn. After enduring month of jokes about their *Honeymooners* namesakes, they decided they might as well get married. When the opportunity to work together beckoned, they moved their family (two girls then seven and nine) to Minnesota, where they accepted their current positions at the shelter. Alice ran the front (administration, budget, public relations) and Ralph handled the back (animal care, management, property maintenance). The home-life division was more intricate.

Ralph put a huge arm around Nick's shoulder. Nick's knees sagged slightly under the weight.

"Your job is very simple. Walk the animals. One at a time. On a leash at all times. Got it?"

Nick nodded again.

"Think so."

Ralph took off his right glove. A jagged scar like a bolt of lightning crossed his palm diagonally. He flexed his fingers slowly.

"You fish?" Ralph asked.

Nick nodded.

"Lobster mostly. Catch and release."

Ralph extended his open hand.

"Welcome to the shelter," he continued. "This could be your destiny."

Nick took his hand.

"It wouldn't surprise me."

Observing carefully as Lena paced in front of her office windows, Sharon rocked back and forth in the doorway to get the timing right, then stepped in to intercept.

"Busy?"

Like a pinball hitting a bumper, Lena immediately reversed direction without uttering a word. Sharon stepped back.

"There's a call."

Lena's path altered to curve around the desk, but still she said nothing.

"It's Cross from Luria Corporation. He's offering one million but he has to know within the hour," Sharon said.

Lena did not pick up the phone, but her pacing became amorphous, though her seemingly haphazard pattern managed to cross beneath every acoustic tile in the ceiling. Sharon stepped back to the door. Before pulling it discreetly closed, she asked: "Do you know the definition of insanity?"

Preston held the punching bag for Lena as best he could. She punched. He ooofed.

"Want to talk about it?" he asked.

"What's there to say I haven't already said a thousand—" Three quick side kicks. Ooof. Ooof. Ooof. "Times."

"Ever wonder where the term sidekick came from?" Preston asked.

Kick punch-punch combination. Ooof. Ooof-Ooof.

"Why can't I hate him?" Lena huffed.

"Apparently the phrase 'Kemo Sabe' wasn't from an actual Indian language."

"It would be so much easier."

"The word was invented by a writer on the *Lone Ranger* television show."

"I hate everyone else."

Punch. Ooof.

"No, you don't."

"No. I don't. Of course I don't. I'm about to be a duly recognized humanitarian."

"You're a what?"

Lena paused, leaning on the bag.

"Nick used to be on the board of directors of I swear every animal welfare and environmental organization in the state. After the divorce, when he dropped out of circulation, I stood in for him temporarily. At least I thought it was temporary. I kept thinking he'd come back eventually. And now they are giving me this award for meritorious humanitarian service to the community."

Preston stepped back.

"I have a surprise," he said.

"What?"

"I found someone to take him."

Lena kicked, missing the bag but not Preston, who collapsed backward. She sailed through and over him, landing on hands and knees facing his feet, with her thighs on either side of his head.

"I'm not exactly sure how to react to this," Preston commented.

Lena didn't move.

"Who?"

Preston didn't move either.

"A group home. A good one."

A crowd of gym shorts loomed above them. Lena carefully extricated herself.

"Really?"

Preston tilted his head off the floor to nod.

"Tell him tonight," he croaked.

From the floor, Lena gave the bag one more punch.

"Don't I always?"

Lena's apartment took up only about two-thirds of the upper floor of her building. The rest was a rooftop balcony, forty-nine feet wide and twenty-three feet deep. Bags of soil, empty planters, and unopened envelopes of seed lay scattered against the wall.

The eastern side of the balcony allowed an early-morning sunrise vigil over the Mississippi River. On the opposite side, the sunset highlighted the silhouette of the cityscape of downtown Minneapolis, shining towers reflecting the evening transmutation like sparkling palaces in the clouds.

Absorbed in that later spectacle, Nick sat on the balcony. On the table next to him, a half-filled wineglass cast back the intensity of the blood-stained horizon. The cloud palaces were burning.

Lena emerged from the balcony doors.

"I thought you weren't supposed to drink when you're taking medication."

Nick raised his glass and adjudicated the luminous show, gauging the process against the cast of the liquid. The clouds flowed to cobalt.

"I'm not."

Lena paused.

"Not what?"

Nick was silent.

"How'd it go at the animal shelter?" Lena continued.

Nick lowered the glass and took a sip.

"They have animals there."

"That would have been my guess."

He looked up at her.

"In cages."

Lena sat next to him and put her hand on his arm. Her fingertips pressed his bicep.

"Nick. You know that the charges against you can be reinstated. If you do anything out of line, you could end up in prison. Or involuntarily committed to a psych ward. This isn't a game."

She removed her hand.

"I'll be good," he nodded. "Want a drink?"

Lena shrugged.

"Sure."

He handed her his glass.

"Did you know that sunset is sunrise backward?" he asked.

They both stared out at the softening light.

"And memory is imagination in reverse," he said.

Lena took a sip, then peered into the glass.

"What is this?"

"Hawaiian Punch."

The phone rang. Lena spun in bed, hesitated, then groped for the receiver.

"What? Oh, hi. No. I couldn't. It's just. He's very fragile now. I know. I know. I'll tell him this morning. I promise. I'll call you later."

Lena threw on her silk robe and went looking for the flannel one to put over it.

In the hallway, she hesitated in front of Nick's door. She reached for the wrought-iron handle, then released it and knocked gently. No answer. She made a hasty check of the hinges, then swung the door open and slipped inside. No one.

On the pillow, she found a note in Nick's scrawl: *There's fresh coffee in the kitchen. See you tonight.*

Lena sat on the side of the bed and pulled back the covers. Sancho was underneath, furry noggin askew on the pillow. Lena slipped under the sheets and snuggled close. She exhaled, then drew the covers up over her head.

Ralph carried the wine crate through the maze of cages, trying not to look at the other animals, and went out through the back door.

The five kittens, probably about six weeks old, had been brought into the shelter thirty days earlier. None had been adopted. Now, according to the rules, none would be. Originally the time limit had been five days. Ralph and Alice had lobbied to expand that to thirty, and management had reluctantly agreed, under the condition that adoptions increase concomitantly.

Behind the shelter, Ralph unlocked the gate, placed the box carefully in the chamber, and sealed it. At the side of the chamber, he twisted a brass lever. Gas hissed inside.

Ralph and Alice had also asked to switch to some of the newer synthetic gases, or possibly to lethal injection. Studies had determined that these methods were faster and produced less stress on the dying animal. Although carbon monoxide gas was generally thought to be effective, there were anecdotal reports of extreme suffering before the animal lapsed into unconsciousness. And more than one handler had died from CO gas poisoning. But the other methods of euthanasia were more expensive or required additional handlers, so the change had not been authorized.

The kittens inhaled the deadly gas. In a few moments, they receded into unconsciousness. Minutes later, their hearts failed. Soon after, all brain function ceased. The fragile remains cooled and constricted.

After fifteen minutes, Ralph unsealed the chamber. According to the recommended procedure, five minutes was all that was necessary. But young animals with tiny lungs sometimes took longer to die.

Ralph removed the crate. The dead kittens were curled up together as if sleeping. He carried the litter to the biological waste disposal container and gently positioned the kittens inside.

Back in the shelter, he removed the gloves, washed his hands, and drifted past the cages to the front lobby. He sat by Alice and held her hand. Neither spoke.

Nick dragged himself into Lena's apartment, exhausted by the efforts of the day. Lena was lying on the sofa, surrounded by a barricade of paper.

"How'd it go?" she asked.

Nick collapsed into a chair.

"It kept going and going. I must have walked a hundred animals today, round and round an asphalt courtyard. I'm still dizzy."

Lena tossed Sancho over to Nick.

"He's been waiting all day," she said.

"I'm exhausted."

"Come on."

"No. No. No. Okay."

Lena picked up the remote control for the stereo.

"Ready?"

Nick stood up and nodded. Lena clicked the remote. "The Liberty Bell" march. Loud.

Nick and Sancho began to march, barely going through the motions. Lena looked at him scornfully.

"Oh, come on."

She joined them, sliding her hands along an imaginary trombone. Nick fingered one-handed an invisible E-flat cornet as Sancho led the way with an Unreal piccolo between his paws.

Around the room.

Over the sofa.

Around the chair.

Into the kitchen.

Around the island.

Between the stools.

Down the hallway.

Into Lena's bedroom.

When the music ended, they collapsed together on the bed, Sancho between them. Nick was breathing hard. Lena laughed between gasps.

"Sometimes," she said in a breathy whisper.

"What?"

She paused.

"Sometimes I miss your world."

They relaxed together, arms touching, breathing in sync. Lena inhaled deeply. She didn't look at him.

"What do *you* miss?" she asked.

Nick didn't answer for a time.

"I miss being annoyed," he replied.

Lena spun around to him.

"Me too!"

Nick continued.

"I miss being awakened at five A.M. by the sound of either a coffee grinder or a dentist's drill, I'm not sure which."

"I miss seeing your footprints in the new-fallen snow and knowing that you are leaving wet tracks all over the oriental carpet."

"I miss the fog of hairspray in the bathroom."

"My hairspray is infused with rare floral essences from the rain forests of Borneo, harvested by an eco-friendly reforestation project

run by the indigenous tribes in the Taman Nasional Danau Senta-
rum in Indonesia. My hairspray is a natural religious experience."

"Can I get an 'amen'?"

She slugged him on the arm.

"Violence begins when imagination fails." He rubbed his bicep,
smiling. "It's the eternal paradox. Love is annoyment."

"Annoyment?" Lena considered. "Is that a word?"

"Questioning my word choice. I miss that too," Nick said, swip-
ing Sancho away from her and setting him on the nightstand.
"That's very annoymentish."

"You're the expert."

"Be it known," Nick declared, "and published in two newspa-
pers of general circulation that we, hereinafter referred to as the De-
fenders of the Innocent, seek no enmity with your kind."

He leaned back and closed his eyes.

"You know what I miss. I miss all of that annoying kissing."

"That was extremely annoying," she agreed.

Nick opened his eyes, looked at her.

"Maybe we should annoy each other."

He leaned closer.

"Right now."

Closer.

"On the lips."

Lena shook her head.

"Absolutely not. Probably not. What was the question?"

Nick kissed her.

"Are you annoyed?" he asked.

"Yes, I am extremely annoymentated."

He tried to kiss her again, but Lena pulled away.

"I think that's all the annoymentacity I can handle. You should get some sleep."

Nick smiled.

"Funny thing is, this is a bed."

Lena smiled back.

"Funny thing is, it's not your bed."

Nick nodded.

"I see your point. Yeah, we're pretty tired. We should get some sleep."

Lena touched his shoulder.

"Isn't it better when the music is real?" she asked.

"The sound comes and goes. The music is always real."

CHAPTER 5

The Wandering Bark

Oscar accelerated in elongated steps down the steep bank, heading in the direction of the lagoon, a narrow finger of water that stretched into the community at the northern end of Lake of the Isles. At the bottom of the decline, he slowed to a stroll and headed across the sward to the inner path, one of two asphalt rings encircling the lakeshore.

Swept up the slender channel on a southern breeze, Nick's voice guided Oscar along the path.

"In the early 1800s," the voice recited, "the chief lumberjack of the northern woods was the legendary giant and frontiersman Paul Bunyan. But one day in the summer of 1836, Paul lifted his head and looked far out over the Minnesota territory and the great forest that he loved. Everywhere he saw the desolation that he and his fellow lumbermen had wreaked. And he realized that the ruin he had caused could never be undone. Devastated by this vision, Paul grew despondent and great tears began to fall from his gigantic eyes."

Ambling past the blue flag iris that emerged still glistening from the green water, Oscar was escorted along the lagoon edge by a squadron of Canada geese, who bowed in concert as they passed the kingfisher perched on a bulrush. Nick's voice still floated toward Oscar like the narration in a nature film.

"For weeks that summer, Paul traveled all over the Minnesota territory, from logging camp to logging camp, from grove to ancient grove, begging forgiveness from the trees he had wronged. But the voices of the trees had been stilled forever by the axes and saws and spikes of the lumbermen. As he walked in silence, ten thousand tears fell across the land, and each tear formed a lake."

When Oscar reached the point where the lagoon flowed into the larger lake and the path turned off to the west, he stopped. Only a slender branch of water, a few yards at most, separated him from the northernmost of the two islands in the lake. One hundred yards across, a morsel of floating life, the island was covered by a chaos of spruce and pine, elm and aspen. A swath of tall grasses swayed along the narrow shore, alternately hiding and revealing the sign from the Minnesota Department of Natural Resources, a warning to would-be picnickers that the island had been set aside as a wildlife preserve.

"Finally, Paul could stand the guilt no longer," the voice continued. "He hurled his gigantic ax south, forming the bed of the Minnesota River. Then he took three giant steps north, creating three lakes: Lake Harriet, Lake Calhoun, and Lake of the Isles.

"At Lake of the Isles, two huge objects fell from Paul's watch chain, forming a pair of small islands in the lake. One was his golden watch, which was larger than the great clock of London. The other was a silver, heart-shaped locket that held a picture of Paul's one true love: Beulah Heatherthorn, the gentle redheaded beauty he had left behind in Erie, Pennsylvania.

"Paul knelt at the top of Lake of the Isles to recover his precious possessions, but the tears so filled his eyes that he could not find them. Finally he took one step west, forming Cedar Lake, and was never seen in Minnesota again. In the summer, if you listen at the northern end of Lake of the Isles, you can still hear the silver locket beat with the sound of Beulah's broken heart and the golden watch tick with the sound of Paul's lost years."

Oscar turned west and followed the path around an embankment. There he found Nick sitting on a park bench set back under the trees. A huge dog was draped over him, trapping Nick on the bench. Sancho balanced between the dog's enormous shoulders. Oblivious to the joggers and bikers and other park denizens circling around him, Nick rocked back and forth and told his stories to the lake.

"I was in the area," Oscar called out. "Thought I'd see how you were doing. Your wife told me you might be here."

Nick started, turned around as far as his canine companions would allow.

"Ex-wife," he corrected mildly.

"I followed your voice," Oscar explained.

"The water does that, I think. Or the wind. I was rehearsing. I might go back to teaching some day."

Oscar looked around.

"Nice spot."

"Welcome to my domain," Nick responded, sweeping his hand broadly across the horizon. The movement stirred the dog, who lifted his head, glanced at Oscar, sniffed once or twice, then returned to drowsy contemplation.

Oscar circled around to the side of the bench.

"So. How are you feeling?" he asked.

"Not wisely but too well," Nick responded.

"What does that mean?"

"It means ask a different question."

Oscar nodded, then turned his earnest attention toward Sancho.

"Nice puppet," he said.

"He prefers Unreal American," Nick replied.

"Oh. Sorry," Oscar said to Sancho. To Nick: "I was surprised they let you keep him at the hospital."

"I made a substantial contribution to the Lunatics' Ball."

"Where did you get him?"

Nick leaned back, extending his long legs and clasping his hands behind his head.

"Once upon a time, I wanted a dog. Lena didn't want a dog. I insisted that we get a dog. So she went out and got Sancho. And that's a brief history of our marriage."

Oscar nodded.

"Is it a boy puppet or a girl puppet?" he inquired.

"He's a him. You want to hold him? He doesn't bite."

"Really? Thanks."

"Often," Nick said.

Oscar gently accepted Sancho.

"He's so soft."

"Inside too. It's okay. He won't mind. He knows you."

Oscar held Sancho's head down and searched for the inner pouch.

"No, not like that," Nick corrected. "Stand up straight. Hold him up over your head. Then slip your whole hand in in one smooth motion, like a knight's gauntlet."

"I see," Oscar replied.

"I call it the Ritual of Joining," Nick explained. "It helps us clear our minds and focus on the mission."

"Kind of like the Green Lantern recharging his ring."

Oscar slipped his hand into the soft inner pouch. His fingers easily found the jaws and paws. Sancho twisted his head back and forth like an owl, intently observing the other park enthusiasts.

"He handles well," said Oscar.

"You should see him on the straightaways."

Oscar nodded, pointed to the huge dog on Nick's lap.

"What's his name?"

"Wolfram."

"Good name. He looks Spanish."

"He's Irish actually."

"That's what I meant. Irish."

"He's an Irish wolfhound. Largest dogs in the world."

Oscar nodded at Sancho.

"How do they get along?"

"Quite well, actually. Sheepdogs and wolfhounds have a lot in common professionally. Speaking of which, why aren't you at the institute?"

Oscar examined the bench, trying to find someplace to sit.

"That's part time, mostly nights, weekends, transport jobs. During the day, I work children's parties."

Nick brightened.

"Are you a clown?"

"I do animal balloons. Here's my card."

Oscar took a business card out of his wallet and handed it to Nick, who read:

THE AMAZING OSCAR

PARTY BALLOONS

BALLOON ANIMALS

PARTY ANIMAL

WWW.AMAZINGOSCAR.COM

"I love balloon animals!"

Oscar took a couple of balloons out of his pocket, blew them up into long, thin cylinders, then twisted them into a hat with antlers. He crowned Nick with it.

"How do I look?" Nick asked.

Oscar offered his professional judgment: "In all my years as a party animal, no adult human has ever looked that good in a moose hat."

"Thanks," said Nick.

"Hey, I have a gig this afternoon. Why don't you come? You could handle the helium. I have this tank. It's easy. And kids love puppets."

"What would we do with him?" Nick said, patting Wolfram's bulky frame.

"We could pretend he's a pony."

Nick shifted under the huge dog until he could take a deep breath. He pointed out toward the lake.

"If you wanted to get to that island," he asked, "how would you do it?"

"Probably I wouldn't. There's a sign."

"I know. I put it there," Nick said. "But if you were going to. How would you?"

"You could swim. Maybe jump. With a running start. Or pole-vault. You could pole-vault."

Nick paused.

"I think I'd walk," he finally decided.

"You know, when I have a tough decision to make, I always ask myself: What would Spiderman do? Or Mister Fantastic. Spiderman was actually kind of neurotic. Which is understandable, I think. The pressures of being a superhero."

"Tell me about it," Nick said.

"Mister Fantastic was married to the Invisible Girl, whose brother was the Human Torch. Makes all the difference. Family. Superman's family was dead. Batman's, dead. Spiderman's, dead. There's a pattern there."

There was a long pause. The grave rhythmic stirring of Wolfram's chest was the only movement.

"When I have a tough decision to make," Nick said, "I always ask myself: What would I do in that situation? It makes it easier somehow."

"Good tip. Aren't you supposed to be walking him?" Oscar asked.

Nick looked at Wolfram.

"He's kind of a Zen dog. He likes to sit and think."

Nick began to sing sotto voce in an Irish accent, so softly that Oscar could barely hear.

" 'For always night and day, I hear lake water lapping with low sounds by the shore; While I stand on the roadway, or on the pavements gray, I hear it in the deep heart's core.' "

Wolfram lifted his shaggy head. Oscar nodded along.

"Did you know that Zen is not a religion?" Oscar asked. "It's a practice, brought to the island of Japan in the twelfth century by a master named Dogon."

Nick looked over.

"*Mystic Existential Ninjas,* Issue 103," Oscar explained.

"You read a lot of graphic novels?"

Oscar snorted. Wolfram's ears jolted skyward.

"That's just a phrase some marketing geek made up so they could charge ten dollars instead of a buck. They're comic books. They were comic books when I was five and they're comic books now."

"I never understood why they were called that," Nick said. "I never thought they were funny."

Oscar's forehead forged a tiny wrinkle between his eyebrows.

"Some people believe they're called comic books because the books in the 1930s were collections of newspaper comic strips. *Terry and the Pirates* and *Dick Tracy* and *Flash Gordon* and *Jungle Jim.* Cervantes wrote the first comic book, you know."

"I'm familiar with it," Nick said.

"The French philosopher Henri Bergson said that comedy is the shared human modality of reacting to the unexpected."

Wolfram stirred.

"He also said comedy requires an unemotional observer. I don't see how those two go together."

Nick nodded.

"Aristotle said that comedy is the celebration of the erotic impulse. Freud thought so too. He said jokes are psychoerotic manifestations of unconscious desires. And Georg Wilhelm Friedrich Hegel, well, he just wasn't funny."

Nick shrugged agreement.

"I think. I think." Oscar looked around, then whispered: "My theory is that comic books are about vision. All superheroes have x-ray vision or some kind of supersenses. That's why comics have all those bright colors."

Nick nodded.

"Thanks for clearing that up."

"There's no telling what you can learn from comics."

Nick picked up Sancho.

"He has supervision."

"Well, he should. He's a puppet."

"No. I mean, he has *super*vision."

"Really?"

"He's a sheepdog," Nick explained.

"So?"

"So he can see who is innocent."

"That's good," Oscar said. "Most sidekicks have lesser powers. I can't think of any sidekicks who have complementary abilities."

"He's not my sidekick. He's my partner."

"Oh. Well. That explains it."

Nick grew pensive for a moment, stroking the soft patch behind Wolfram's ear.

"What does an existential ninja do?" he asked finally.

"Nothing," Oscar replied. "It's what he *could* do."

"Ahhhh."

Oscar squeezed in, joining Nick and Wolfram on the bench. They sat without talking and watched the activities along the lakeshore.

Children played.

Dogs chased.

Geese swam.

Squirrels browsed in a never-ending quest.

Oscar passed his hand over Wolfram's shaggy coat.

"Smart dog."

The birthday party was being held in the backyard of a large house in north Minneapolis. Wearing the balloon antlers as his official badge, Nick arrived early with Oscar, passing under the party streamers hung in kaleidoscopic arches along the hedges. As promised, Nick helped blow up the balloons, helium specials that spun "Happy Birthday Jeremy" in the warm southern breeze.

Diminutive guests and attendant adults arrived in erratic procession. As the party commenced, Nick, Sancho, and Wolfram faded into the background to watch.

Oscar truly was Amazing. To the delight of the onlookers old and young, animal balloon sculptures soon filled the yard. There was a red-and-blue monkey holding something like a banana, a long yellow-and-green snake coiled and rising into the air, and even a purple-and-orange giraffe that stood almost six feet high. Nick insisted from the back that Oscar put glasses on it. The children turned and discovered him there, with Sancho.

The five-year-olds looked expectantly at the man with the puppet. Nick raised Sancho into the air and slid his hand inside.

The puppet lifted his head slowly and rubbed his eyes. Then he spotted the children and danced for joy. Nick harrumphed. Sancho turned and gazed at Nick for a long time. Then he dipped his shaggy head between his paws and shook it back and forth. The children hooted with laughter.

"Tell us a story!" they commanded.

Nick shook his head.

"Once upon a time," Oscar prompted.

Nick glanced around at the multicolored zoo Oscar had created, drew a big breath, and stepped forward.

"In the heart of a lake in the heart of a city in the heart of a land in the heart of the world there is an island in the shape of a heart.

"The island is home to many amazing animals: a purple-and-orange giraffe who recites poetry, a red-and-blue monkey who plays the saxophone, and even a yellow-and-green snake who juggles. But none is more amazing than the Magical Dog Who Never Sleeps. The Magical Dog forever stands on guard on the shore of the island.

"One fine sunny morning, a Knight in Blue Armor comes riding along through the forest and sees the island. And he thinks: 'Any island in the shape of a heart with a nearsighted purple-and-orange giraffe, a red-and-blue monkey who plays the saxophone, a yellow-and-green snake who can juggle, and a Magical Dog Who Never Sleeps must be a wonderful place indeed.'

"So the Blue Knight calls out, 'Oh, wise and wondrous Magical Dog, how may I get onto your island?'

"The Magical Dog replies, because all Magical Dogs can talk, 'Memory in reverse is Imagination.'

"'Hmmm,' says the Blue Knight. 'Should I swim to the island? Should I jump? Should I pole-vault?'

"But the Magical Dog only says again: 'Memory in reverse is Imagination.'

"'Ahhh,' thinks the Blue Knight. Then he kneels down by the water's edge and, seeing his reflection in the calm, shiny surface, dips his right hand through the image, lifts the water up in his palm, then casts the glittering droplets up into the air. Suddenly a rainbow stretches from the shore of the lake all the way onto the island. Then the Blue Knight stands and walks over the rainbow bridge onto the enchanted island.

"And the Blue Knight abides on the island in the shape of a heart while the purple-and-orange giraffe recites poetry, while the red-and-blue monkey plays marching songs, while the yellow-and-green snake juggles two pomegranates, a teacup, and the knight's very sharp sword. Finally the Blue Knight thinks that it must be time to leave, so he says: 'Oh wise and wondrous Magical Dog, this is a very fine island, but how does one get off?'

" 'Beats me,' the Magical Dog replies. 'Why do you think I'm still here?'

" 'No. Seriously,' says the Blue Knight.

"So the Magical Dog laughs and says: 'Imagination in reverse is Memory.'

"And so the Blue Knight kneels down once more at the water's edge and dips his left hand into his image and again casts the glistening droplets into the air. Once more a rainbow appears, and the Blue Knight crosses back over the many-colored bridge onto the lakeshore.

"But when the Blue Knight turns to say good-bye, he sees himself still standing on the island. So he asks the Magical Dog: 'Oh, wise and wondrous Magical Dog, why do I see myself still standing on the island next to you?'

"And the Magical Dog replies: 'On this island, there is no time. No day. No night. No past. No future. There isn't even any Now. There is only Always. If you are ever here, you are always here.'

"And the Blue Knight replies: 'Then I won't say good-bye,' and he turns and walks away.

"The End."

Nick and Sancho turned and walked away underneath the streamers.

"Who wants to ride the pony?" Oscar asked quickly.

Lena stood inside the door for a few moments as Nick and Sancho patrolled the perimeter of the balcony to a tune no one else could hear. Finally she stepped out.

"There's something I have to tell you," she said.

Nick turned to her.

"There's something I have to tell *you*," he responded.

Lena sat quickly and covered her eyes with her hands.

"I knew it. We're not really divorced, are we?" she said.

"Of course we're divorced," Nick replied, sitting next to her.

She uncovered her eyes.

"Sorry. My mind always jumps to the worst possibility."

"Thanks a lot. I was—"

"You slept with someone while we were married."

"No. I didn't sleep with anyone while we were married. That was part of the problem. What is the matter with you?"

"I'm just. I don't know. There's something I have to tell you."

"I know what we need," Nick announced, leaping to his feet.

"No."

"We need—"

"No!"

Nick lifted his right arm with a flourish.

"A balcony scene!"

"Oh no."

He knelt at Lena's feet, took her hand, kissed it.

"'Let me not to the marriage of true minds admit impediments,'" he exclaimed.

Lena pulled her hand back.

"No Shakespeare."

Nick rushed to the balcony railing, draping himself against it.

"'Love is not love which alters when it alteration finds.'"

He spun over the balcony railing, clinging to the iron trestle by his fingers and toes.

"'Or bends with the remover to remove.'"

Flakes of paint rotored their way down thirty-some feet to the rocky ground below as the antique bolts began to wrench loose from the floor.

"Nick!" Lena pleaded.

Nick raised up on his toes, as though preparing to leap.

"'O no!'"

"Oh no!"

He vaulted onto the thin line of the railing. His voice dropped in volume.

"'It is an ever-fixèd mark that looks on tempests and is never shaken.'"

Lena turned away. Nick inched slowly down the slender rail into her peripheral view. He spoke to the river: "'It is the star to every wand'ring bark.'"

A step.

"'Whose worth's unknown.'"

A step.

"'Although his height be taken.'"

On the last word, Nick lost his footing. Lena screamed at his flailing shadow. But Nick caught himself, twisted in onto the balcony floor, rolled over to her and up, kneeling again.

"Ow. 'Love's not Time's fool,' ow, 'though rosy lips and cheeks within his bending sickle's compass come.'"

Nick waited. He waited for a long time. A minute. Two. Lena did not look at him, but finally muttered: "'Love alters not with his brief hours and weeks, but bears it out ev'n to the edge of doom.'"

Nick lowered his head into her lap.

"'If this be error and upon me proved, I never writ, nor no man ever loved.'"

Lena pulled back, slid out, swept away, then halted in the doorway.

"Every time the phone rings, my first thought is that someone has found you somewhere, dead. My first thought. Every time."

Nick looked up at her. She stood just inside the doorway. The interior light flickered, revealing and concealing her silhouette.

"Is that a good thought or a bad thought?" he asked.

"Yes," she answered and vanished inside.

Nick picked up Sancho and stood at the railing.

"Any given sunset."

The phone woke Lena, who stared, then grabbed for it.

"Where is he? Oh. Hi. I was dreaming, I guess. No, I couldn't tell him. I just. Yes. Lunch. I can meet you."

Nick was preparing to walk his charges for the day when Ralph entered the cage room wearing wet gear, a poncho and boots. He threw a set to Nick.

"Put those on."

"Why?"

"Field trip."

Nick and Ralph left the shelter and climbed into a white van.

"Where are we going?" Nick asked.

"Not far. A pair of geese has decided to take up residence in someone's swimming pool."

"Not the mayor's, I hope."

"You know the mayor?"

"We're acquainted."

As the van pulled out, Nick shimmied into the slick outerwear.

"Who else keeps a swimming pool in Minnesota?" he asked.

Ralph shrugged.

"An optimist."

Fifteen minutes later, the van pulled up to a large house in southwest Minneapolis not far from Lake of the Isles. Ralph trudged around to the back of the van and opened the panel doors.

"So how are we supposed to catch these geese?" Nick asked.

"You'll see."

After searching a while, Ralph pulled out two long poles with nets and a flat vinyl case.

"What do we do with them after we catch them?" Nick asked.

"They're big birds."

"That's why I'm asking."

"So generally I like to roast them at medium heat for five or six hours."

Nick put his hand on Ralph's shoulder. Ralph turned.

"You eat them?"

"We relocate them."

Nick took the poles.

"I won't kill anything."

Ralph nodded solemnly.

"For your sake, I hope the geese feel the same way."

Ralph passed through a gate in the hedge at the side of the house. Nick followed him into an enormous yard, almost a park. The pool was located near the house, up from the English garden. About ten yards long, the blue cement pool was encircled by a raised white concrete walk surrounded by a weathered brick patio. In the deep end of the pool, farthest from the gate, two Canada geese cruised gracefully, unperturbed by the approaching men and equipment.

"They mate for life, you know," Nick said.

Ralph took one of the nets.

"So do humans. They just don't admit it as often."

Ralph strolled calmly but quickly over to the smaller of the two birds. He extended the pole and netted the goose without a struggle. Then he carefully drew the uncomplaining bird to the edge of the pool.

"That was easy," Nick said in admiration.

Ralph reached down, pulled the goose out of the net, and handed her to Nick.

"Be careful. She'll bite your ear off."

"I know the type," Nick replied.

The goose held still for a moment. Then a shudder ran through it up into Nick's arms, causing him to loosen his grip. Wings freed, the sturdy pinions assailed Nick vigorously, showering him, almost blinding him in feathers. Teetering on the cement ledge of the pool, Nick held the bird as far away from his body as possible, pulled on point several times by the frantic aviator.

"Careful," Ralph warned. "Those wings can break your nose."

"You tell me that now?"

The struggling goose squawked in alarm, at which point the mate, terrified and honking also, rose out of the water into the sky, circled the pool for momentum, and dived at Nick, who lost his grip on the captured goose and ducked too far. For one photo-finish second, he posed in peril, then toppled in stiff slow motion into the water. He breached the surface like a harpooned whale, stole a quick breath, then belly flopped once more into the pool.

Ralph extended the pole to Nick's grasping fingers and dragged him to the side.

"They mate for life, you know," Ralph commented.

As the pair of geese settled calmly once again into the deep end, Nick tried to shake himself dry. Ralph opened the black vinyl case and pulled out a small pistol with a long, thin barrel. He took practiced aim at one of the geese and fired the air-driven missile.

Without a thought Nick launched himself across the pool, arms extended, trying to get in front of the projectile. Once more he plunged in, then struggled up in knee-deep water. Drenched and woozy, he tried to focus on the tiny dart protruding from his palm. He saluted Ralph, lofting his hand like a kid parading a newfound penny.

Ralph nodded, impassive.

"They told me you were funny."

Nick barked a laugh as he slipped back into the cool fluid blue.

Preston approached Lena's table at the restaurant, maintaining as much momentum as possible while winding through the narrow passages between mostly empty tables. When he reached her, he didn't sit.

"Why haven't you told him yet?"

"Sit down."

He glared at her.

"Please," she said.

"I pulled a lot of strings to set up this group home for him on such short notice."

"Will you please sit down? People are staring."

Preston glanced at the patrons scattered sparsely through the restaurant and decided to sit. He leaned across the table.

"He'll be better off. And you'll be better off."

Lena folded her hands on the table in front of her. Preston waited.

"I don't know how to explain it," she said finally.

"You never changed the message on your answering machine," Preston accused.

"I don't like the sound of my voice."

"Do you feel guilty?"

"You know, Nick would have a field day with that line."

"Just because you divorced him."

" 'Sound of my voice.' "

"And took over his legal practice."

"He would have riffed for an hour."

"And he had a complete mental breakdown?"

"Yes!" Lena cried. "It's my fault. It's my fault. It's my fault," pounding the table, causing waves in the water glasses and eliciting stares.

Preston held up his hands to calm her.

"That's not true."

Lena shook her head.

"He's mentally ill, Preston. He's disabled, for God's sake."

"He's a nut."

"I left him."

"That's why they call them nuts."

"It's as if—"

"Because they crack."

Lena shot up out of her chair.

"My husband was in a wheelchair and I pushed him down the stairs!"

A gasp made its way around the room, then with Midwestern discretion the customers hid their heads in their menus. Preston took Lena's hand.

"Will you sit down?"

He lured her back into her chair.

"You did the right thing," Preston said. "The divorce was necessary. Your being together wasn't helping either one of you. The marriage was over."

"Right."

"He was acting crazy. Spending money crazy. Accepting crazy cases. You and the firm would both have gone bankrupt."

"Right. Right," Lena agreed.

"He isn't the man you married anymore. It's tragic but you have to think of him as gone and not coming back. People with this disease don't get better, and if they did, they still wouldn't be who they were before."

Lena ran her hands through her hair.

"But what if he can't make it?" she asked. "I don't think he can make it."

Preston took both of her hands this time.

"The captain does not have to go down with the ship, Lena. The captain is a beautiful, compassionate, valuable person that I, that I care about. Her job is to do her best and then save herself. Did you do your best?"

"I hope so."

"Then keep repeating: 'I have a right to my own happiness.'"

"I have a right to my own vodka. I need a drink."

Preston signaled their waiter, Stanley.

"Something is happening between us."

"Us?" Preston asked.

Lena shook her head.

"Nick and me," she said.

Preston jumped out of his seat.

"Not that, Preston," Lena reassured him. "I don't think."

Preston sat again.

"You don't think?" he hissed.

Stanley placed the drinks on the table.

"These are compliments of the manager. He asked if you would please stay in your seats. You're scaring the tourists."

Preston looked around.

"What tourists?"

Stanley shrugged.

"Okay, you're scaring me. Just keep it down. Please?"

Nick woke up soaking wet in a dark, damp, quivering metal cave. Two geese snoozed next to him, wings pinioned. Ralph was driving the van. Nick scooted up toward the front.

"Where are we?"

Ralph twisted partway around in the driver's seat.

"On our way to geese paradise."

"Which I hope is not someplace named paté."

Ralph turned back to the front.

"Trust me."

Nick shrugged.

"Well, you've inspired me so far. Why shouldn't I trust you?"

"You know, I thought you would have recognized a tranquilizer gun."

"Silly me. How did you get the geese in the truck?"

"I dumped you in and they just followed right after."

"Really?"

"Yep. Oh. I put some towels in the back. You know. Just in case."

After a lunch spent mostly in silence, Lena gazed into one of several empty glasses. Staring through the thick lens of the glass bottom, she watched Preston's face shrivel and warp and sink into the distant haze.

"I need to understand what is going on," Preston said quietly.

Sunlight shone and scattered through Lena's empty glass, refracting an oblong pattern on the white tablecloth: two flattened rainbows joined at each end.

"I have done everything I know how to do," she said.

She aimed the rainbows at Preston, at his pale shirt, then up his pale tie to his pale face.

"When he gets in trouble," she said slowly, groping for the words, "I'm the first one there. Other than the ambulance. Or the fire department."

"Or the SWAT team," Preston added.

Lena beamed the rainbows like a tiny spotlight across the finger where her wedding ring used to be.

"Nothing I do is—"

She paused.

"Enough," Preston added. "He uses your feelings to keep you from letting go."

Lena shook her head.

"You don't know him," she said.

"Do you?"

Preston moved his chair next to hers.

"Let me take care of you. And him," he said.

"How?"

"I'll find a way."

Lena put down the glass. The rainbows disappeared. She put her hand over Preston's.

"I'm so sorry for putting you through this," she said.

"There's nothing I wouldn't do for you."

The Minneapolis skyline was no longer visible through the rear window of the van. Nick lay quietly in the back, watching the geese, who had awakened and were watching him back.

"Trust me," he whispered.

The van soon pulled off the highway onto a dirt road. Branches lashed the windshield until the lunging vehicle halted, then backed up briefly.

Ralph turned around.

"We're here."

Nick slid toward the back and opened the doors. A wide meadow of flowers and tall grasses ran about a hundred yards down to the shore of a lake maybe half a mile across. Except for the small clearing, evergreens formed an impenetrable bulwark above the sturdy fortress of trunks. No trace of humanity was visible.

Ralph appeared at the back of the van and helped Nick out. Nick stood unsteadily on the ground, his leg muscles shaky and cramped, as a company of geese soared over the van and plunged onto the watery surface with a rainbow spray.

"I told you," Ralph said. "Geese paradise."

Nick reached into the truck and handed the geese one by one to Ralph, who held them at arm's length as he placed them gently on the ground. Nick knelt down beside them to deliver last-minute instructions.

"This is your new home. You'll be safe here. None of those irritating humans around to pester you," he said, glancing at Ralph.

Ralph knelt and freed the first bird. The powerful avian extended his wings and ran a few wobbly steps, then glided up and out over the lake. Nick hurried to free the second, having learned never to impede a mating goose. The pair sailed side by side in a graceful arc over the trees, then circled the two men before landing in the lake with a glittering shower.

Nick whispered: " 'Beautiful bird; thou voyagest to thine home, where thy sweet mate will twine her downy neck with thine, and welcome thy return with eyes bright in the lustre of their own fond joy.' "

"What was that?" Ralph asked.

Nick shrugged.

"Shelley."

Ralph nodded.

"Amen."

Lena doodled mindlessly across a stack of important papers until Sharon casually pulled them away from her.

"Cross from Luria Corporation called again," Sharon said. "He's offering two million."

"I'm not here."

"I said you were."

"It's a mirage."

"It's Minnesota."

"It's snow blindness."

"It's summer."

"It's Minnesota."

"It's two million."

"I'll get back to him."

Sharon perched on the steel arm of the sofa.

"How was lunch?"

"I'm not hungry."

Lena pulled the papers back, picked up a pen, and began filling in the holes in the o's and p's and d's, damming the alphabet, as Nick called it, so the meaning can't escape. She had often complained about this habit of his, especially when she discovered the marks in papers about to be filed in court. Only recently had she discovered how satisfying it could be.

"Why don't you go home to your ex-husband?" Sharon asked.

Lena checked her watch.

"Can't. He's out saving the world."

Sharon leaned against the bookcase.

"I wish I had an ex-husband to not go home to."

"You want mine?"

Sharon struck her best Doris Day pose.

"You don't know what you're not missing."

Lena put down the pen and drifted over to the windows. To the west, city towers gave way to houses and apartments that gave way to lakes and parks then to farms and deserts and forests and mountains. The incline of the West. Civilization in reverse.

Sharon moved in at the desk and helpfully continued to fill in the holes in the letters. Lena spoke to the window.

"Nick used to send me roses. I don't know where he got them. He would never say. Deep crimson, they were called, but the color of the petals changed depending on the light. Under fluorescent light they looked black, outside in the sun blood red. At dusk they looked like a burgundy wine. I'd put them in a crystal vase on my desk and the whole room would seem like it was on fire.

"One day Nick bought me a dozen. Then he remembered I was out of town. So he chartered a jet to deliver them. I was in Geneva at the time. The Swiss customs agent apparently had a hard time believing someone would charter a jet just to deliver a dozen roses. So for eighty-nine thousand dollars, I got a pile of crushed petals and twelve sticks with thorns. When I got home, I filed for divorce. And that's a brief history of our marriage."

Sharon picked up the document and turned it to see whether it made more sense upside down.

"He meant well," Sharon noted.

"So did Karl Marx."

"Was he the one with the cigar?" she asked, doing an imitation with the pen. Lena walked back to the desk.

"I never heard of anyone getting divorced over roses before," Sharon continued.

"That was when, not why."

"So why?"

"Don't you have some work to not do?"

"I already didn't do it."

Lena slid open the glass door to the condo balcony, expecting to find Nick. The declining sun cast stark elongated shadows over the weathered planks. None she recognized.

The van pulled up to the shelter. Nick and Ralph began to unload the gear.

"You did good today," Ralph noted.

"That's what I live to hear."

"Why don't you come home with me for dinner?"

"This is so sudden."

"Alice will have everything ready."

"Okay," Nick agreed. "Let me make a call."

Lena reclined on the balcony, sipping a glass of wine. A small candle held out alone against the night. Her phone rang. She waited, then answered it.

"I wondered where you were. I'm here watching your sunset. Or I was. No, it's okay. Whenever. It's not house arrest. Just be quiet coming in. Yeah. Bye."

She hung up, blew out the candle, and went inside, closing the glass door behind her.

Ralph and Nick rolled to a stop in front of a house on Minnehaha Parkway. The four-story Victorian seemed to be built into a hill. Ralph led the way up the stairs to a moss-green veranda lined with buttercup-yellow gingerbread. Ralph swung the door open and walked into a kiss from the waiting Alice, who then granted Nick a peck on the cheek. Nick stood frozen by the unexpected pleasantry. A second later, all three were inundated by dogs.

"We've adopted a few over the years," Ralph explained.

Lena lay on the sofa in a powder-pink cotton nightshirt, papers scattered around her, working. Her knees were drawn up beneath the nightshirt, hiding nearly all of her thick red socks. She alternated handfuls of Cheerios out of the box with sips of milk from a champagne flute. Her hair was captured in two long braids. Sancho perched on top of the sofa, supervising the activities.

Lena clicked on her small tape recorder and began to dictate: "Sharon, here are the notes for my speech at the London Convention.

"Title Identity and the Rights of Children new paragraph In the 1990 UN Convention on the Rights of the Child comma Article 8 defines the right of a child to preserve his or her identity without unlawful interference period But what constitutes that identity question mark The convention cites three elementary criteria of identity colon nationality comma name comma and family relations period But what else question mark What makes a child this child question mark Even our child question mark new paragraph To understand this comma we must examine how the law identifies a person period Under the law comma identity does not mean identical period A person is never the same as he or she was the day before comma either physically or psychologically period Cells grow and die by the millions each day period We gain weight or lose weight by the minute it seems period We add and lose memories in the same way period Our neurological pathways are continually altered by the sensible input we receive comma and by the internal feedback system that we refer to as ourselves comma our consciousness period new paragraph."

She stopped the tape and listened. Then she put down the tape recorder and reached for the remote control on the coffee table. The CD player clicked on: "The Liberty Bell" march. She tuned the volume very low and turned her attention to her papers. Her toes, emerging from beneath the nightshirt, marched to the music.

Ralph, Alice, and Nick pushed back from the table simultaneously. The dinner plates were empty.

"Thank you for a delicious meal," Nick offered.

"I noticed that you formed your mashed potatoes into a pyramid," Ralph mentioned.

"It helps the butter melt evenly," Nick explained.

"You didn't try the chicken," Alice remarked.

"I don't eat meat."

"How long have you been a vegetarian?"

"About five hours."

Alice's eyes grew wide.

"Actually," Nick continued, "I'm a geometrarian."

"What is that?" Ralph asked.

"I only consume foods in elementary shapes. Like circles or rectangles or pyramids."

Alice relaxed back into her chair.

Nick went on: "Someone once tried to convince me that broccoli florets grow in Fibonacci sequences. But for me, pure mathematics ended with Euclid."

Ralph leaned forward.

"Plus I don't like broccoli," Nick finished.

He smiled.

Then Alice smiled.

And finally Ralph smiled, then rumbled out a chuckle, then thundered a laugh that shook the condiments.

Nick looked through the doorway into the living room and spotted a piano. He turned to Alice.

"You play?"

Alice nodded at Ralph, who said with some embarrassment: "I play at it."

"He's good," Alice countered. "He plays every Tuesday night with some friends down at a little jazz club."

"Jazz?" Nick said. "Would you?" he added, nodding toward the piano.

"Go ahead," Alice told Ralph. "I'll get the dishes."

"Thanks, hon," Ralph replied. Then to Nick: "Good thing you're here. Dishes are usually my job."

"You two are so different," Nick said after Alice went into the kitchen. "And you're together all day and all night. How do you make it work?"

Ralph put his finger to his lips.

"Duct tape and Krazy Glue. I'll say no more," he replied.

Ralph and Nick crossed to the family room. Ralph sat at the piano and touched his fingers lightly to the keys.

"A good marriage," he continued, "is not a democracy. It is a series of contiguous tyrannies by mutual consent."

Ralph's hands curled into something slow and syncopated.

"Ahhhh," Nick responded.

"Marriage," Ralph announced, "is a partnership sustained by a common vision."

"How do you know?" asked Nick.

"She told me so," Ralph replied.

Ralph turned toward the kitchen.

"It's not always like this," Ralph added with warmth. "But it's like this enough."

Alice wandered in. Her hands, always busy with something, were now wringing a dishcloth.

"You like music?" she asked Nick.

"I love it," Nick responded.

"Who's your favorite?"

Nick stood at reverent attention.

"John Philip Sousa."

Ralph and Alice nodded but kept quiet. Ralph lifted "Stardust" to march time.

Lena woke to see Nick sitting on her bed.

"Sorry," he said. "I didn't mean to wake you."

She put her head back down.

"What time is it?"

Nick checked the clock beside her bed.

"It's tomorrow."

"Tomorrow," Lena slurred, trying to remember something. "Tomorrow. Tomorrow. You have an appointment with . . ."

"Dr. Richardson, I know."

"He has to file a report with the . . ."

"Court, I know. Go back to sleep."

He pulled the comforter up.

"What are you going to do?" she asked the pillow.

"I missed my sunset. I thought I'd watch you for a while."

"No. You. Okay. Good-night."

Nick settled back on the bed and pulled Sancho to him.

Lena felt pressure on her leg and woke suddenly. Nick was curled up asleep at the foot of the bed, his arm draped awkwardly over her thigh. Lena got up carefully so as not to wake him.

When the alarm went off, Nick jumped and rolled onto the floor. When he looked up, he saw Sancho with the alarm clock in his lap. Nick shook his head.

"Traitor."

CHAPTER 6

Tempests

Nick leaned back in the chair. Sancho, riding on his lap, nearly tumbled off, but Nick caught him.

Dr. Richardson got out a notepad and sat down across from Nick.

"You don't have any books here," Nick noted.

"I can't read," the doctor replied. "So, how are you feeling?"

"Not wisely but too well."

The doctor closed his notepad.

"You know, maybe I didn't explain this properly, but therapy generally includes talking about yourself."

Nick considered.

"No, thanks."

He slid his hand up into Sancho's interior. Dr. Richardson turned his attention to the puppet.

Sancho moved leisurely at first, as if waking from sleep. He yawned. He scratched. His dark eyes scanned the room.

Dr. Richardson observed with careful curiosity: *The naturalness is uncanny, his control is effortless, as if his hand has somehow grown a consciousness of its own, a separate awareness, a distinct intention. He pays no attention to the puppet's actions at all, except when they are directed at him. An extraordinary performance: detailed, consistent, convincing. And slightly unnerving.*

The puppet who had become Sancho turned toward Dr. Richardson. The cherry tongue appeared as the jaws widened in a smile. The doctor found himself smiling back.

"Tell me about the puppet," Richardson said.

"Once upon a time, I wanted a dog. Lena didn't want a dog. I insisted that we get a dog. So she went out and got Sancho. And that's a brief history of our marriage."

Richardson nodded and smiled.

"Good name for a sidekick."

"He's not—I didn't name him. Lena did."

"Why did she pick that name?"

"It's a mystery."

The doctor returned the smile.

"You two spend a lot of time together?"

"We're divorced."

"I meant you and Sancho."

"We're just good friends."

The doctor laughed.

"You like him."

Nick and Sancho turned to each other.

"He's the best person I know."

"You talk as if he's real."

"Real is trickier than people realize."

The doctor laughed again, tasted his pen, then changed the subject.

"Staying on the meds?" he asked.

"Usually. Sometimes. Not really," Nick admitted finally under the doctor's gaze.

"I see."

"Do you ever watch movies on PBS?" Nick asked.

"Occasionally," said Richardson. "*Mystery.* The wildlife programs."

"You know how for a movie they put those black borders on the top and bottom?"

Nick held his palms outward, one over his forehead and one below his chin.

"That's what my brain feels like when I take the pills," he added.

Richardson made another note.

"Try and think of it as editing for *Prime Time.* We just take out the bad parts."

"You mean the exciting parts."

"I mean the dangerous parts."

"I'll try to remember that," Nick assured him.

Richardson paused, drumming the pad with the pen.

It's the job. To cure. So. Throw medication and therapy at the problems like politicians throw money. Maybe, somehow, the right buttons will get pushed. We have theories: dysfunctional families, dysfunctional neurotransmitters, sanity as chemistry. But our theories don't begin to approach the complexity of brain function. Not to mention mind function. And the soul? We pray it's not there. What pill can ever cure a soul?

During the doctor's silence, Nick's usually animated expression swallowed itself, three dimensions folding into one solemn surface. His eyes reflected sky as he focused out the window.

"What's going to happen to me?" he asked finally.

"Well, let's see," the doctor replied, going back over his notes. "You have a serious mental disorder. You're divorced. You have no job. You don't take your medication. My guess is you'll be dead in five years."

Nick shifted in the chair.

"Haven't you ever heard of a rhetorical question?"

"Sorry," the doctor replied.

Nick glared at the doctor.

"I'm not crazy," he whispered.

"We don't say that word here. We think it a lot but we don't say it."

"I'm not crazy," Nick repeated firmly.

The doctor leaned forward, gazing intently at Nick.

"No?" he challenged. "Then what are you?"

At the question, Sancho swiveled, cocked his ears, and gazed at Nick with equivalent intensity. Nick shrugged.

"I am. Imaginative."

The doctor nodded and scribbled in the notepad.

"So it would seem."

"So what do I do?" Nick asked.

"Was that rhetorical?"

"No."

"Well, one choice would be to take your medication, stay in therapy, and get your imagination under control."

Nick thought a moment.

"What's the second choice?"

Richardson closed his notepad.

"Make it a good five years."

Lena arranged the elephants on her desk in Traveling Circus order, alternating large and small. All of them had names, but only
Lena knew what they were.

Names. Identity. Names. What is a name? What's in a name?
A rose by. No. No roses. Forget roses. Nick. What's in a Nick. A Nick
is a nick is a nick. The knack of Nick. We don't really know. We don't
really know who we are as much as we remember ourselves. Our
stream of consciousness flows into an ocean of memory and by this
memory, this correlated continuous database of personality and hap-
penstance, we awake each day to reconstruct ourselves in the real
world. Whether this reconstruction is the same is an issue, like the
teleporter in a Star Trek *episode: when Captain Kirk is beamed up to*
the deck of the Enterprise, *is he the same person he was on the surface*
of the planet? I wonder if our dreamselves have memories just as our
conscious minds do? And if the lives of the dreamselves (and who
knows how many there are) affect our bodies the way we do? If so, I
hope my dreamself goes to the gym more often than I do.

Lena didn't notice when Sharon entered the office.

"Cross is on the phone again," Sharon announced. "He's offering three million plus future royalties. He says to please call him
back at your convenience."

Lena didn't respond.

Sharon walked to Lena's desk, pulled on the headset, and, in her
best Lena imitation, announced into the phone: "Cross? Lena Grant.
Three million plus royalties, and I want the fucking check on my fucking desk by the end of the fucking day. Thanks for fucking calling."

Then she hung up on him.

"Want some fucking coffee?" Sharon inquired.

As Nick strolled into the shelter, he noticed that Alice was not at her appointed place. Instead, Preston Winter sat behind her desk reviewing some papers.

"Doing your own investigating," Nick said. "I'm flattered."

"I've taken a personal interest in your case," Preston noted.

"How am I doing?"

"Surprisingly well, unfortunately."

Nick crossed his arms.

"Do you enjoy what you do, Preston?"

"The pay is low, but the benefits are good and I get to have people killed."

"I'm happy for you," Nick said. "Where is everybody?"

"Back with the veterinarian. Some dog is sick."

Nick rushed toward the cage room.

"See you later, Preston."

"You certainly will," Preston agreed as he stuffed papers into his briefcase.

Back in the cage room, Nick found Ralph standing outside Wolfram's enclosure, looking worried. Nick hurried up beside him.

Wolfram was lying on the floor of his cage, his breathing labored and shallow. A veterinarian knelt by him. Alice stood by his side.

"We found him like this early this morning," she said.

"Will he be okay?" Nick asked the vet.

"Don't know," the vet responded. "He's been in a cage for a month. That's hard for an old dog, especially one his size."

"He's been here a month?" Nick asked.

"Come day after tomorrow," Alice told him after a quick glance at Ralph.

"So. So what do we do?"

Alice shook her head but the vet responded: "We wait. Call me if anything changes."

The vet packed up and left.

"He's a great dog," Nick said to Ralph. "I'm surprised he's been here so long."

"He's old and he eats like a horse. People don't want a dog like that," said Alice.

Wolfram lifted his great head off the floor to see Nick, then tried to get up but couldn't. He lay back down, struggling to breathe.

"Okay if I stay with him?" Nick asked.

"Sure," said Ralph and Alice simultaneously.

Ralph looked back in. Nick was sitting on the floor with Wolfram, his hand across the dog's neck.

"Any change?" Ralph asked.

Nick shook his head.

Alice's figure filled the door of Wolfram's cage. Nick and Ralph had moved a little table and a couple of folding chairs into the cage. They were sitting next to Wolfram, playing chess.

Alice shook her head.

The overhead lights went on. Alice reappeared at the door to the cage. Nick and Ralph were still playing chess.

"Thought you could use some illumination," Alice offered.

"It's a popular opinion," Nick replied.

Nick and Alice were at the chessboard. Ralph dozed on the blanket next to Wolfram. Both were taking smooth, shallow breaths until Ralph stirred.

"What time is it?" he asked, blinking away the bleariness.

"Almost midnight," Alice replied.

"Why don't you two go home?" Nick offered. "I'll call you if anything changes."

Alice considered and nodded.

"Anything, you call us."

Ralph and Alice left. Nick brought in a small lamp from one of the unused front offices, then switched off the overhead fixtures. The tiny lamp formed a circle of light on the floor. Nick relaxed on the old blanket next to the huge hound, pulled out his cell phone, and dialed Lena.

"Hi. I was pretending you were worried so I could call and tell you not to be worried. One of the dogs is sick. I'm going to stay. I don't know, could be all night. Sleep well. Bye."

Nick looked at Wolfram, who had awakened and shifted his head across Nick's knees.

"Do you play chess?"

Lena opened the steel door to the cage room. She was wearing an old sweatshirt and tights, a St. Louis Cardinals baseball cap, a ponytail, and white sneakers. She passed under a rainbow of streamers and balloons and wandered down the first row of cages adorned with Day-Glo posters. In the dim light, she strained to read the message on each.

Watson: A male bloodhound mix, Watson loves long walks on the beach in search of anything.

Alonzo: This spaniel male was neutered while training for an Olympic fencing medal. He loves children, riding in the car, and the films of Frank Capra.

Fanny: A wily Alsatian female best known for her impersonations of French cabaret singers of the 1950s.

Pal: Beagle puppy. He's a puppy. Everybody loves puppies.

Rufus: This male sheepdog/husky mix is a champion chaser who can find a tennis ball in any kind of weather. Rufus is housebroken and prefers Plato in the original Greek.

Grendel: This female shepherd mix needs no leash and loves other pets. She recently saved Timmy from a burning barn.

Annabelle: Female schnauzer mix. A loving mother of twenty-seven, since retired, Annabelle has a wild side and can frolic through a meadow with the best of them.

Huck: Labrador retriever–mix male. Sweet-natured and very playful, Huck is a wonderful swimmer, loves to play in water, and recently received critical acclaim for his existential novel Woof!

Wolfram: This well-fed male wolfhound is quiet and compassionate with children and possesses knowledge beyond human understanding.

She found Nick in the last and largest cage, sitting on Wolfram's blanket with one hand across the huge dog's neck.

"You look like a sixteen-year-old escaping to spend the evening with her boyfriend," Nick commented.

"I was bored all alone," Lena replied. "So I thought I'd come down and be bored with you."

Nick lifted his arm. Lena slid under it, resting her head on his chest.

"By the way, you don't play chess," she said.

He nodded.

"That explains so much."

Nick opened his eyes and promptly shut them again. The morning sun shone starkly bright even through the dingy windows above his head. He tried to stretch his cramped legs but found himself trapped. A sleeping Lena suffused his lap in a fall of strawberry blond. Wolfram dozed with his snout across Nick's knees.

Ralph walked in.

"A ménage à trois," he said, eyebrows raised. Nick looked down at his sleeping charges.

"In a menagerie no less," Nick replied.

Lena opened her eyes, stood up, and stretched.

"I'm Lena," she said, offering Ralph her hand.

"Ralph."

Lena nudged Nick with her foot.

"I have to get to the office."

"Thanks for being bored with me," Nick said. Lena nudged him again.

"It was a first," she said and ambled down the aisle, drawing every male to attention, regardless of species. At the double door, she turned and waved. Ralph looked at Nick, who hadn't stirred.

"You let her go?"

"It was a mutual decision. No, it was more like mutually assured destruction."

Ralph stooped to check Wolfram, ran his hand over the still form. Wolfram hadn't yet lifted his head.

"No change?"

"Not much."

"Well, it's probably just as well. Tomorrow is E day."

"E day. What's that? We send him somewhere?"

"In a way."

Nick slid his legs from under the dog and rolled onto his knees to face the big man.

"What?"

"E is for Euthanasia."

"You're going to kill him?"

"Policy. If they haven't been adopted in a month, then . . ."

Nick looked back at Wolfram.

"You can't be serious."

"A month is a lot. In many shelters, they get only a few days. Let me show you something."

Ralph stood and hauled Nick to his feet, then led him to the rear of the shelter and out the back door. Ralph opened the gate, walked inside, and put his hand on the gas canister.

"This is carbon monoxide. It produces unconsciousness in seconds. They just go to sleep."

"How do you stand this?" Nick asked. "You love these animals. I know you do."

"It's for their own good," Ralph argued. "Is it better for them to run around loose, starving to death, hurting someone or hurting themselves?"

"Some people say the same thing about me," Nick said. "I can't believe this goes on here. This is Minneapolis. The capital of Nice. There must be some other way."

"You don't understand the issues," Ralph tried to explain, his own voice rising. "Neutering and adoption programs don't come close to solving the problem. Millions of animals every year come into shelters all over the country. Where would we put them? What would we do with them? People want brand-name pets. They don't want generics."

Nick shuddered.

"I can't let this happen," he said decisively.

"We've been here for fifteen years," Ralph said. "You think we haven't tried to change this? Change it if you can. Too bad you're not still a lawyer. I bet you knew the governor personally."

Nick walked back inside and slid onto the floor, his back against a cage. Ralph sat beside him. For a while, nothing was said.

"I've had years to learn to deal with this," Ralph said. "You're a good man, Nick. Don't come around tomorrow."

Ralph stood, waited a moment, and walked away. Nick watched him recede, then stood rapidly and quick-marched out front. Alice was sitting at the desk. He raced past her without speaking.

"Hey?" she asked.

Nick ignored her, banged open the front door, and walked out.

Lena was on the sofa, holding Sancho on her lap.

The legal fiction of identity reaches past our ever-changing stream of physicality and personality to seek that which is, if not the same, at least continuous. We identify a person physically by external ap-

pearance. In criminal procedure, we have the eyewitness and the ubiquitous lineup. We hold each other responsible for the actions that are performed by a body. But we have found that for real identity we need to look deeper, or differently. We look to handwriting or fingerprints or DNA. But even this is not conclusive, because the law also recognizes in rare instances a multitude of identities within a single body: the multiple personality, the insane individual who is not in possession of his or her faculties. Not in possession. If we are not, who is?

It was late when Nick dragged himself into the apartment. He wandered aimlessly for a few seconds, then slumped into his chair. Lena waited for him to speak. He didn't.

"Bad day?" she asked.

He didn't answer.

"Want to talk?" she prompted.

Nick turned his face to her without really looking at her. After a second, he stood and walked back into his bedroom. Lena heard the door click softly shut.

"We never talk anymore," she murmured.

She cleared up her work and followed him back to his bedroom. She put her ear to the door, listening for a moment, then opened it. Nick lay on the bed, holding Sancho, staring at the ceiling.

"Alice called," Lena said. "She told me."

Nick didn't turn to her, but kept staring up.

"Do you know how many animals are euthanized in animal shelters each year? Do you have any idea?"

Lena sat next to Nick on the bed.

"No," she said.

He didn't look at her.

"Neither did I. And tomorrow, it's Wolfram."

Lena braced his shoulders and pulled him around to face her.

"There's nothing you can do," she said, then softened. "I'm sorry."

Expression drained from Nick's face. He pulled away from her and walked to the window.

"I can't do nothing."

"I'm speaking as your attorney," Lena said.

"Are you?"

She didn't respond.

"We could adopt him," Nick said.

"I can't have this discussion."

"I'm just saying."

"There is no *we*, Nick."

Nick stiffened and tucked himself safely away.

"We'll figure out something," he said.

Lena shook her head, started to speak, stopped, then turned and left the room.

Nick pulled a card out of his wallet, then picked up the phone and dialed.

"Oscar? It's Nick. I need your help. The Minions of Euthanasia must be thwarted by the Agents of Anthropomorphosis."

Lena lay on her bed. She heard a door slam, got up and opened hers. Nick's door was wide open. His room was empty. She closed her bedroom door and sank down against it.

In the morning, she opened Nick's door a crack, then pushed it wide. He was on his bed, dressed, or still dressed.

"Morning," Lena said.

"Morning."

She stepped into the room.

"When did you get in?"

"Late. Sorry."

"Aren't you going to the shelter today?"

"It's E day. They said stay home."

Lena put her hand on his shoulder. He didn't pull away.

"Call me if you need anything."

He didn't respond.

"I'm sorry, Nick. I really am."

Nick shrugged.

"It's life. Or not."

Alice sat at her desk. Ralph sat nearby.

"You may as well get it over with," Alice said.

Ralph walked reluctantly back through the shelter, stopping at Wolfram's cage. The old dog looked up. His tail wagged briefly.

"Soon it won't hurt anymore."

Ralph knelt down and slid his green leather gloves under Wolfram's frame. His muscles surged and he curled the dog against his chest, lifted one knee then the other, and stood. He shuffled slowly to the back door of the shelter and out, struggling under the weight of the massive canine. At the exit, Ralph froze in place. The gate leading to the chamber stood open.

Attached to the chamber itself, a balloon floated. The logo read:

KILLING IS EASY

Then the other side flipped around in the breeze, and Ralph read:

COMEDY IS HARD

Ralph shook his head as he lowered Wolfram gently to the ground. The huge snout lifted into the air and sniffed, sensing something not right.

Ralph untied the balloon and watched as it drifted up in a slow spiral, out of the enclosure, over the fence and trees, disappearing finally in the morning sun. Then he squatted down to test the chamber, twisting the handle on the gas canister.

A blast spurted in his face. He inhaled involuntarily. Gasping, he looked at the canister.

The rubber hose had been cut.

He backed away, coughing, and shouted for help.

"Alice!"

Ralph's voice didn't carry. It sounded odd. Higher in pitch. Registers higher. Wolfram lifted his head and howled.

Ralph looked again at the gas canister. The label said HELIUM.

"What the hell?" he squeaked. "Alice!"

Ralph looked up to where the balloon had flown and laughed out loud. To Wolfram, he announced in a chipmunk voice: "Well, old boy, I guess you get a reprieve."

Lena stormed through her front door, slamming it behind her.

"Nick!"

She threw off her jacket and purse and charged into the living room.

"Nick!"

She headed down the hallway to his bedroom. She didn't knock this time but threw the door back on its hinges, punching an S-shaped dent in the wall with the antique door handle.

Nick and Sancho were on the bed watching CNN.

"I had to!" he explained.

"Helium? You substituted helium?"

"I'm playing for time."

"Where did you get helium?"

"Minneapolis is a party town. You can get the stuff on any street corner: balloons, streamers, cone hats, whatever you need."

Lena sat on the bed.

"Alice had no choice," she told him. "She had to report to her boss, who called the judge. The charges have been reinstated and the judge has ordered you back to the institute. You have to turn yourself in tomorrow. You're going to be involuntarily committed or go to prison. There's nothing I can do."

Nick smiled.

"You never support any of my projects," he said.

Lena spun away in fury.

"I hope you can laugh when that door slams shut on the next ten years of your life."

"Good thing I've only got five years to live."

Lena shook her head.

"You know, it just occurred to me. You always say that I left you. But the truth is, you left me first. Every time you avoided the issue or dived into the remote control or told a joke instead of talking to me, you put one foot out the door."

Nick paused, then: "I must have had a lot of feet."

Lena nodded, shrugged, rose slowly, and moved to the door.

"Who do you love?" Nick asked softly when her back was turned.

The question caught her.

"You mean 'whom.'"

"I know the difference."

She turned.

He was looking directly at her, not accusing, not penetrating, merely posing, as if he were her professor again, as though the answer were academically intriguing but nothing more.

"I don't understand," Lena said after a moment.

"No, I don't think you do," Nick agreed. "But then maybe I don't either."

"Are you asking about Preston?"

"No."

"Then?"

Nick sat up, put Sancho to the side.

"Who do you love?"

She leaned her head against the door, eyes concealed in a curtain of blond hair.

"I don't know who you are anymore."

"We are who we imagine. So are you."

Her hand curved tightly around the door handle.

"I don't know what you're trying to tell me."

Her wrist twisted. The door clicked open.

"Wait," Nick said.

She turned back once more to find Sancho hurtling through the air to her. She caught him and held on.

"You shouldn't be alone tonight," Nick said.

"You're right. I shouldn't."

She left the room, not slamming the door but closing it tightly.

Nick began to pack his few things, stuffing them hard into a suitcase. Before he finished, he slumped on the bed.

The door creaked. He looked up.

"You shouldn't be alone tonight either," she said.

Lena and Nick lay in bed.

"That was unbelievably annoying," Nick said.

Lena tipped his face toward her. Her eyes mirrored darkly in his blue. She shifted up high on the bed so she could look down at his face.

"They say the definition of insanity is doing the same thing over and over again and expecting a different result."

"I don't expect anything."

He pulled her down.

Lena sat on the washing machine, naked and sweaty, leaning against Nick.

"That's what I like," she whispered in his ear.

"What?"

"Extra starch."

She began to giggle.

Nick pulled back and gaped at her.

"Our last minutes together and you're telling jokes?" he asked. He wiped away a pretended tear. "I'm so proud."

Too exhausted to laugh himself, he still managed carry her back to the bedroom.

When we read a book, our minds, our minds assemble the words and spaces and punctuation into a text, and our imagination assembles bits of text into a character. In life our minds assemble the elements of experience (words, looks, touches, actions) into memories, and from those memories our imagination constructs a persona. Even those we love exist only in our imagination. Only. Only . . .

Lena and Nick lay in her bed, eyes closed. She rolled over to him, her head pressing his chest.

"I just want you to know."

"Yes?"

"I just do."

"Okay."

She eyed the shuttered windows for a sense of sunrise.

CHAPTER 7

The Bending Sickle

Nick kept forgetting about the handcuffs, dragging one hand with the other as he chatted amiably with the police officers. He knew them; they were friends who often stopped to swap stories as he circled Lake of the Isles. He was their neighborhood watch, as the squirrels and geese were his.

The police car circled through the parking lot, heading for the emergency entrance to the Golden Valley Psychiatric Institute. The officers opened the rear door, carefully helped Nick out, and escorted him inside.

Oscar was waiting, dressed again in his lab coat, a ravaged *Spiderman Versus The Rhino* hanging out of the left pocket. He removed Nick's restraints quickly, all too aware that escape was impossible. Oscar recognized the ancient forms. Protasis. Epitasis. Catastasis. Catastrophe. The Old Ones knew. Sophocles. Horace. Stan Lee. Jack Kirby. The Mighty Thor No. 154 to No. 157, the greatest comic epic of the modern era. The Mangog, last survivor of a holocaust and imbued with the power of a billion billion extinguished souls, seeks to bring about Ragnarock, the end of days. Now Ends the Universe. The God of Thunder fights, is defeated, rises again, and foils the enemy with the aid of his faithful companions.

The forms ruled.

Comic books.

No telling.

Oscar led Nick through the labyrinth of bland back corridors, into the elevator to the ninth floor, through the locked doors, and back to his room.

Nick lay down on the tiny bed.

"Sorry, Nick," Oscar said and shut the door with a muffled deadwood thud.

Nick started from sleep as Lena dropped her briefcase on the tiny white table. She tossed the puppet to him.

"We need to prepare your testimony for the competency hearing tomorrow," she said, not waiting this time for Nick to speak first. He raised his right hand.

"I solemnly swear to tell the truth, the whole truth, or nothing but the truth."

Lena grabbed a gavel out of her briefcase and banged the table, just missing Nick's left hand.

"That's '*and* nothing but the truth,'" she amended.

"Can't I just pick one?"

Lena removed a legal pad and pen from her briefcase, slipped off her shoes, and leaned precariously backward on the two rear legs of the chair, resting her feet on the bed.

"What were you doing at Lund's grocery store on June 11?" Lena asked.

Nick picked up the puppet and began to pantomime the events.

"We were on a routine training mission. Suddenly things got hot. We spotted the perp assaulting the victims, so we identified ourselves and attempted to intervene."

"Training for what?"

"Defending the innocent."

"And why do you do that?"

Nick lifted Sancho like a stone tablet.

"And God said: 'Behold the Defender of the Innocent. Unless you shall be as one of these, you shall not enter the kingdom of heaven.'"

"Did he say this to you in person?"

"Of course not."

"Good."

"It was on C-SPAN."

Lena nodded to Sancho.

"Why him?"

"He's a sheepdog."

"So?"

"He can see who is innocent."

Lena put down her notebook and pen.

"You can see whether someone is innocent?"

"I can't. He can."

Lena leaned forward to look at Nick. Sancho leaned forward to kiss Lena on the forehead with his fuzzy pink tongue.

"How. Does he. What?" she asked.

Sancho stood at attention and saluted with his paw.

"Love," Nick replied.

"You can see that?"

"I can't. He can."

She drew his conclusion.

"So if I loved you, I would be considered innocent?"

"By reason of insanity."

"I'll take your word on that."

"Thank you, Ms. Grant," Nick said and turned to Sancho. "No more questions."

Lena closed her notebook.

"Nick. If this goes beyond tomorrow, beyond the competency hearing, we need to find you a new lawyer. It's not smart for me to represent you."

"Can't decide whether you want me to win?"

"No," she said. "I can decide."

Nick waited. Then Sancho's paw pointed to Lena.

"We want you," Nick announced.

Sancho nodded vigorously.

"May I come in?"

The voice belonged to Preston Winter.

The bedsprings groaned as Nick sat up.

"Be my guest," Nick said. "Or am I yours? I forget."

Preston sat in the chair and leaned in over the wobbly wooden table.

"I've decided to put you out of your misery."

"But you just got here," Nick responded pleasantly.

Preston continued, unwilling to interrupt his rehearsed speech.

"I can't see Lena hurt this way any longer. I'm going to end her suffering. And yours."

Nick folded his arms. "Our tax dollars at work."

Preston paused. "You object to euthanasia?"

Nick nodded. "Too many syllables."

The lids of Preston's eyes lowered slightly. He would not lose control, despite the intense turmoil. The stakes were high. An ex parte communication could cost him his job. He knew Nick knew that. What he was about to propose could cost him everything, or win it.

"It's from the Greek, you know. It means 'a good death.' "

"Why are you here?" Nick asked.

"You're a smart guy, Nick. I thought, maybe, you would do the right thing."

Preston moved next to Nick.

"Look at this place. Imagine a lifetime in here, a lifetime of drugs and restraints and therapy and more drugs until finally there's no you anymore. You're gone. And as bad as this place is, prison is worse. Much worse. You know that. You've seen it."

He edged closer.

"Imagine what it will be like for Lena with you here or in prison. You lose. I lose. She loses."

Nick put his arm around Preston's shoulder and escorted him the few paces to the door.

"I wouldn't watch any more *Godfather* reruns if I were you, Preston."

Preston smiled.

"Your family will be taken care of."

He stopped smiling.

"Take care of yourself, Nick."

Preston and Lena spoke quietly outside the courtroom doors.

"They're adding charges. Destroying government property. Interfering with a government operation. Reckless endangerment."

Lena's mind raced.

"Those are felony counts."

Preston nodded. "They think he's some kind of animal rights terrorist," he added.

"They want jail time?"

"No deals. He's committed or he goes to jail."

"Can't you do anything?"

Preston shook his head.

"If the judge rules that he's competent, he's going to prison," he told her.

Lena began pacing in front of the doors.

"You're telling me that to keep him out of prison, I have to commit him to a mental institution."

"Yes. The judge must decide that he is unable to stand trial. If that happens, commitment is a certainty."

"It won't work. Whatever I try, he'll see through it."

Preston's expression was brittle.

"Not if he still loves you."

Lena collapsed on a bench.

"How can I do that to him?"

Preston edged down next to her.

"Maybe you shouldn't," Preston answered firmly.

Lena shot him a trapped look.

"How can I not?"

Oscar escorted Nick into the same small courtroom that had been used for the arraignment. Like pieces on a chessboard, they moved into the previous diagonal juxtaposition.

Sharon sauntered through the courtroom doors, pulling a litigation case behind her. She set it on the table where Nick was sitting and then took a seat in the gallery not far from Oscar. She eyed Oscar and the handcuffs with curiosity. Oscar pulled out *Daredevil* 106, which he had folded twice and stuffed into his back pocket. Sharon moved closer.

"Vintage Marvel," she noted.

"You like comic books?" Oscar asked.

"I love them. I'm a big Mr. Fantastic fan," she replied.

Oscar reached into his pocket, pulled out a business card, and handed it to her.

"How amazing are you?" she asked.

A dog barked.

Nick spun around.

Wolfram was sitting by the door, shoulder high to a very nervous bailiff. Attached to his collar, a helium balloon fluttered in the air conditioning. The logo read: BREAK A LEG.

Nick waved to Wolfram, then to Ralph, who was sitting in the aisle seat, barely able to restrain the colossal dog, and then to Alice, seated next to Ralph. Ralph petted Wolfram and gave Nick a thumbs-up. Alice shook a finger at Nick and edged the corners of her mouth into an anxious smile.

Preston and Lena strode into the courtroom together, pacing briskly down the center aisle, bursting in unison through the gate, then splitting at right angles like a marching band from a very small school that couldn't afford any instruments.

Lena edged in next to Nick at the defendant's table. Preston sat at the prosecutor's table. Both looked grim.

Nick turned to Lena.

She shook her head.

He looked away.

Lena took out some papers, then set her watch on the table. The bailiff stood.

"All rise."

Nick recognized Judge Anne Ritchfield from the arraignment.

"Sit sit sit," she ordered, shuffling through her papers, then surveying the hearing room before motioning for the bailiff.

"There's a dog in the courtroom," the judge whispered.

"Yes, Your Honor," replied the bailiff.

"This one looks real."

"Yes, Your Honor."

"Don't tell me: he's a material witness."

The bailiff nodded. The judge sighed.

"Call the case."

The bailiff turned to the court.

"State versus Nicholas Ward."

"Well, I see we're all here once again," said the judge. "Wait. Where's the puppet?"

"Oh!" said Lena, reaching into her litigation case and extracting Sancho. Nick reached for him immediately.

"I want to remind everyone," the judge declared, "that this is a competency hearing, not a trial. Which means I make up the rules as I go along. You can object if you like but don't expect me to care. Any objections?"

"Your Honor," Lena began, standing. She got halfway out of the chair.

"No?" the judge interrupted. "Good. Call the first witness."

Preston began to stand, then looked at Lena, who was frozen in a halfway standing position that to Oscar resembled the Egyptian hieroglyph for indecision. For a moment, Lena and Preston were a silent calliope, sitting and standing, until finally Lena slid into her seat and Preston attained full height.

"The state calls Dr. Henry Richardson," he announced.

Dr. Richardson entered the courtroom briskly and took the witness stand. The bailiff approached him.

"Do you solemnly swear to tell the truth, the whole truth, and nothing but the truth?"

Dr. Richardson did. Preston, hoping to proceed quickly, remained at the prosecutor's table and discharged his questions with pace and precision.

"Doctor, you are a psychiatrist?"

"Yes. In practice for twenty-one years."

"And you are treating the defendant?"

"Yes."

"Have you formed a medical opinion about the defendant's mental condition?

Dr. Richardson looked at Nick.

"Mr. Ward suffers from a psychiatric condition known as delusional disorder."

"Can you describe that for the court?"

Dr. Richardson straightened his tie, after which his hands dropped down to the railing in front of the witness box. His fingers played with an imaginary cigar.

"Certainly. Patients with this disorder have beliefs that they maintain regardless of compelling evidence to the contrary."

"Thank you, Doctor. In your opinion, is the defendant competent to understand the charges against him?"

Dr. Richardson paused.

"Mr. Ward is highly intelligent, often lucid, and his legal knowledge seems, so far as a layman can judge, intact."

Preston stood and emerged slowly from behind the table to highlight his most important question.

"Again, in your professional opinion, is the defendant able to participate in his own defense?"

The doctor paused again, longer this time. His face was troubled.

"That is a much more difficult question. His condition is not predictable and can change rapidly."

The judge broke in.

"Doctor, is Mr. Ward's condition controllable by medication?"

This time the doctor answered quickly.

"Medication can be helpful. There are whole new classes of antipsychotic drugs that might be efficacious. But in Mr. Ward's case, extended hospitalization may be required to find a medical regimen that will consistently alleviate the symptoms."

The judge nodded. Preston stepped up.

"I have no more questions, Your Honor."

The judge looked at Lena.

"Your witness, Ms. Grant."

Lena stood and smoothed out the front of her suit. Her hands were trembling slightly.

"Hello, Doctor," Lena said pleasantly. "I have a simple question. What's wrong with him?"

The doctor said in his wisest voice: "As I said, my diagnosis at this time is delusional disorder."

"Is that what is wrong with him?"

Dr. Richardson looked at Nick, hoping for either a clue or a dispensation. He found neither one in Nick's eyes, which reflected only amused curiosity.

For twenty-one years, Dr. Richardson had dealt with the most difficult of institutionalized cases. Too many of his patients were like Greek tragedies: good people with a fatal genetic flaw that would ultimately destroy not only their own lives but the lives of those around them. He did what he could. Sometimes it worked. Sometimes it worked for a while. Often it didn't work at all.

"That's what we're telling the insurance company."

"So basically he's crazy."

"We don't—"

"Is that why he drives me crazy?"

"It's not—"

"Is there some crazy bug? How is it transmitted? Sexual contact? A sneeze? Gravitation?"

"Counselor," the judge cautioned.

"The German philosopher Immanuel Kant—"

"Why doesn't he love me enough to be normal?"

"Counselor."

It was a question Richardson had heard many times, in many forms. His only answer was another question.

"If he were normal, would you love him?"

Lena glanced at Nick, knowing the answer but unwilling to give voice to it. She stepped away and walked a shaky path back to the defendant's table.

"One last question, Doctor. Could stress be a factor in setting off the delusions? For example, the stress of a trial?"

"Very likely. Stress is often a critical factor," the doctor responded.

"That's all," said Lena as she sat.

"Thank you, Doctor," the judge said. "You may step down." Dr. Richardson took a seat in the gallery close to Nick.

Lena glanced at Preston and nodded, then looked to the judge.

"Your Honor, may we approach?" she asked.

The judge waved them forward. As Preston and Lena reached the bench, Nick leaned down, removed something from Lena's litigation case, and passed it surreptitiously to Oscar.

"Your Honor," Lena said. "I feel that both the state and my client would be best served if he were in a place where he could receive proper treatment for his illness."

The judge stopped her.

"Ms. Grant, I only have one decision to make here today: whether your client is competent to stand trial."

"Your Honor, he talks to a puppet."

"Ms. Grant, do you have stuffed animals?

"Well, yes."

"Do you ever talk to them?"

"Well. Yes."

"I talk to my car," said the judge. "My son talks to the dog. My husband yells at the football players on television. Sometimes he even waits for them to answer. Yet, except for my son, that does not seem to preclude any of us from acting competently."

"No, Your Honor," Lena agreed reluctantly.

"I need proof. Step back."

Lena and Preston stepped back in tandem. Lena turned to him.

"I have to do this?" she asked without hope.

"He'll be better off."

"There's no other way?" Lena asked again, searching Preston's eyes for bureaucratic salvation. Preston shook his head.

"Well," Lena sighed, "what wife wouldn't jump at the chance to drive her ex-husband crazy?"

The judge waived the bailiff over.

"What happened to the dog?" she asked.

The bailiff scanned the room. Wolfram was missing.

"Maybe it went for a walk," he replied.

"Well, if it's not here when it's called to testify, you're in trouble."

"Yes, Your Honor," the bailiff responded.

"Ms. Grant, let's get going," the judge called out. "We only get two weeks of summer here. I'd like to enjoy them."

Lena nodded. "Your Honor," she asked, "may I have a minute to confer with my co-counsel—I mean my client?"

"Any objection?" the judge asked Preston.

"No, Your Honor."

"Make it fast," the judge ordered.

Lena walked over to Nick and leaned across the table.

"It wasn't a dog," she said.

"What?"

"That story you tell: you wanted a dog, I didn't, you insisted, I bought Sancho. It's a good story. But it's not true."

Nick shook his head.

"I don't understand—"

"You didn't want a dog."

"I don't—"

"You wanted a child."

"I—"

"I didn't buy Sancho. You did. You bought a new stuffed animal every day. And every day I tried to imagine what life would be like for our child."

Lena touched Nick's cheek. She could almost hear the drums in his mind begin to roll and the piccolo to trill.

"You're an amazing man, Nick. You're brilliant and funny and surprising in so many ways. You do so many things so well. But I'm just not sure that love is one of those things."

She took her hand away but would not look down.

"And I couldn't do that," she said. "I couldn't have our child go through life feeling the way I felt."

She took a breath.

"So I told you I wanted a child too. Just not with you."

Lena felt, with the professional certainty of one who performs such acts for a living, that she had broken him again, just as she was certain now that she had broken him before with the same statement. And she marked the moment in her mind with the color that she reserved for those acts for which she could not forgive herself.

Nick picked up Sancho. One side of his mouth curled up as he bent to whisper to her: "We are. Imaginary."

He cradled Sancho as he walked away, then carefully balanced the puppet on the dark polished railing as he sat in the witness stand.

"Ms. Grant," the judge said. "Are you ready to proceed?"

Lena turned hastily to the judge.

"I call Nicholas Ward to the stand."

The bailiff approached Nick.

"Please stand and raise your right hand."

Nick stood. The puppet tumbled off the polished railing down to the floor. As the bailiff leaned over to pick him up, Nick calmly slid the weapon out of the bailiff's holster. The bailiff felt the motion, grabbed, but too late. Nick raised the hand with the gun, barrel pointing at the ceiling.

"I solemnly swear to tell the truth, the whole truth, and nothing but the truth. All of the above."

The bailiff stood still, unwilling to move.

"Thanks. I'll take him," Nick said as he retrieved Sancho. "You can go," he directed calmly, motioning the stunned bailiff back with the weapon. The bailiff glanced at the judge, then complied. All other motion in the courtroom had ceased.

Lena fought her shock and confusion, gathered herself.

"Nick, are you crazy?"

He smiled.

"Why do people keep asking me that?"

Underneath Nick's familiar tone she recognized something new and struggled to classify it.

"Put down the gun," she ordered.

As Nick shoved the cold mouth of the gun barrel hard against his temple, he turned to Preston, who stared, unbelieving, mouth half open.

"What we need here is a good death," Nick announced calmly. He surveyed the room and observed the diversity of expression.

Ralph: wondering if it was all a joke.

Alice: worried that she had known it all along.

Preston: shocked and guilty.

Dr. Richardson: unsurprised and riveted.

Oscar: protective of Sharon.

Sharon: protective of Lena.

The judge: powerless and angry.

And finally Lena: terrified but undefeated.

Nick continued: "I mean, it's our proposal. Our method. Our Solution."

Nick went on, his voice quiet, reasonable, chilling: "Inconvenience deserves a death sentence."

Nick turned toward the judge without removing the barrel from his temple.

"But let's not shut it away this time. Let's not hide it in an animal shelter or slaughterhouse or nursing home or prison cell or concentration camp. Let's get it out in the open where we can see once and for all exactly what we are responsible for."

He ran his hand along the slick mahogany surface of the judge's bench.

"Where better for this sacrifice than here?"

Nick waited for an answer. Finally Preston spoke.

"Put it down, Nick," he said. "That's not what she wants. It's not what anyone wants."

Lena glanced around for help, to the judge, to the doctor, to Oscar, to Preston. No one moved.

Finally she looked at Nick. The picture she saw was preposterous and her mind rebelled. Nick hated guns, had never held a gun in his life. She closed her eyes and tried to bring the world into focus again.

All she could think was how sad Sancho would be.

With that image, she sensed the entropy of the universe reverse itself as the fragments of Nick fused in her consciousness and the shattered mirror was whole again.

She took a step toward Nick, holding his eyes with hers, willing him into conjoint awareness. Preston lunged out to pull her back but halted at Nick's warning glance.

"There's something I have to tell you," Lena said quietly.

She continued a step, her voice little more than a whisper: "'Whenever any species is listed as a threatened species pursuant to subsection (c) of this section, the Secretary shall issue such regulations as is deemed necessary and advisable to provide for the conservation of such species. The Secretary may by regulation prohibit with respect to any threatened species any act prohibited under section 1538(a)(1) of Title 16 Chapter 35 of the US Code in the case of fish or wildlife.'"

A step.

"'The term "fish or wildlife" means any member of the animal kingdom, including without limitation any mammal, fish, bird (including any migratory, nonmigratory, or endangered bird for which protection is also afforded by treaty or other international agreement), amphibian, reptile, mollusk, crustacean, arthropod or other invertebrate, and includes any part, product, egg, or offspring thereof.'"

A step.

Inches away.

She put her hand on his arm, imagining her three fingertips like pebbles tossed in a lake, radiating concentric waves of love and serenity through his arm, torso, heart, mind.

Nick cocked his head, tipping the gun barrel up into the air.

"Are you pregnant?"

Lena tipped her head to match his.

"Are you crazy?"

The gun slipped to the floor as he answered: "No more questions."

Nick sank without another word into the witness chair, giving Sancho, who was now in Lena's arms, a brief nod. The bailiff quickly retrieved the gun and handcuffed Nick. The judge peered at Preston.

"Cross-examination, Mr. Winter?"

Preston shook his head.

"Bailiff. Take Mr. Ward to his seat."

The bailiff escorted Nick to the defendant's table. Oscar moved up and sat next to him.

"We rest, Your Honor," Lena said.

"If counsels will waive closing remarks?" the judge asked.

Lena and Preston nodded. Judge Ritchfield continued: "Mr. Ward, medical testimony and other evidence indicate that you have an uncontrolled mental illness that prevents you from fully participating in your defense. The court finds that you are not competent to stand trial on these charges."

Oscar clapped. Nick seemed not to register the remarks. Lena looked down. Preston looked unhappy.

The judge went on: "The court also finds that this condition renders you a danger to yourself and to others. Consequently, I am ordering you confined to an appropriate psychiatric institution until such time as medical evidence shows your illness to be under control. Good luck, Mr. Ward. Court is adjourned."

The judge stood and quickly left the hearing room. Lena took Nick's hand.

"Oscar will bring you out front. I'll meet you there."

Preston's eyes followed Lena to the door, then he gazed at Nick with a puzzled expression. He spun around behind the prosecutor's table, staring at the wall. Oscar escorted Nick out of the courtroom, flanked by a couple of bailiffs.

"Is it all set?" Nick asked in a whisper.

"All set," Oscar replied.

Outside the courthouse, Nick and Oscar waited by the rear door of the institute van. Lena soon emerged from the building with Sancho, followed closely by Sharon.

Nick whispered to Oscar: "I need to speak to Lena alone."

Oscar spoke to the bailiffs, who agreed, but continued to watch Nick closely. Nick gestured Lena into the shadow of the court building.

"I have that stupid awards banquet tonight," she said hurriedly, "But I'll be over first thing tomorrow."

He took her hands as best he could with his wrists restrained.

"You think this is your fault, don't you?"

Lena shouted "Yes" inside but responded: "No."

"Well, it is," Nick said.

Lena was speechless.

"You saved me," he continued.

Lena shook her head.

"You know you're going back to the institute, don't you?" she asked.

Nick laughed. A car pulled up behind Lena. Before she could turn to see who it was, Nick drew her close.

"I have a favor to ask you," he whispered.

"What?"

"I want you to take care of Sancho."

"Why?"

"He's a puppet."

"So?"

"Well, he can't take care of himself."

Lena looked down, then nodded.

"Sure," she said, laughing, unsurprised finally that with everything that had happened this was what he worried about.

"Do you know what this means?" he asked.

"Is it absolutely necessary?"

"You are now officially a Defender of the Innocent."

Nick kissed her on both cheeks like a legionnaire, then lingered on her mouth.

"Thanks," he said.

"There's that word again."

Lena and Nick rejoined Oscar, who was conversing intently with Sharon at the back of the van. Oscar reached for Lena's hand, deposited something cold in her palm.

"I assume this means I don't get the Porsche," Oscar said.

Lena gave him a puzzled glance, then examined his gift.

"These are my car keys. How did you—"

"Time to go," Nick said, climbing into the back of the hospital van.

Sharon moved close to Lena, never taking her eyes off Oscar.

"Do you know the definition of insanity?" Sharon asked.

"Yes," said Lena. "It starts with an L."

Sharon nodded.

"By the way," she said, looking over Lena's shoulder, "nice dog."

Lena twisted around. Her Porsche was parked behind her, top down. In the passenger seat, towering over the windshield, sat Wolfram, observing all with blessed serenity.

"Oh, no."

She turned back to Nick.

"Oh, no!"

Oscar slammed the rear door of the van. Nick waved through the window.

"You. I am not. There is no way."

The van pulled slowly away.

"Come back here!" Lena cried.

Finally she approached the colossal hound.

"Do you remember me?" she asked sweetly.

"Are you hungry?

"Are you really a dog?"

Sipping a snifter of Hawaiian Punch, Lena sat in the lotus position in her office chair (her outfit for the evening hanging behind her). Her desk had absorbed the sunset radiating through the windows, a Turner skyscape enshrined in crystal. The reflection transfigured the walls, entrancing her. Blue to yellow. Sunrise backward. Orange to red. A rainbow smeared out over time. Blue to violet. The happy refraction of the reality circling in the dark.

She tried to identify the moment when the color changed. But she couldn't.

There was no moment of change.

Only change revealed.

The banquet room was full, seats occupied mostly, but not entirely, by women. On the wall behind the dais, the banner proclaimed:

MINNESOTA BUSINESS WOMEN
HUMANITARIAN AWARD

Preston Winter hurried into the room and found Lena seated on the dais next to the podium. He caught her eye, waved her over.

"Something has happened." Lena said flatly. Not a question.

"He's missing," Preston replied. "And so is the van from the institute. And so is the driver."

Lena moved unsteadily. She didn't make it all the way to the chair, but collapsed onto the steps of the dais. Preston knelt beside her.

"He wouldn't hurt anyone," she said.

"After what we saw in court today, can you be sure?"

"I'll come with you," she said. "I know where to look."

Preston took her hand.

"No. I called Harvey. He's helping us look. You go home in case he calls. If he contacts you, call me immediately."

A gray-haired woman in a long gown moved to the podium. Lena saw her, gestured to Preston to wait, and returned to her seat.

"Thank you all for coming tonight," the speaker announced jovially, "and for helping us honor the winner of this year's Minnesota Humanitarian Award. As you know, the award is given each year to the nominee who does the most to make the rest of us feel guilty."

A smattering of laughter rippled through the crowd. Preston sat by the side of the dais.

"Tonight's honoree certainly qualifies with her constant dedication to charitable causes throughout the city, the state, the nation, and the world. Please join me in welcoming tonight's Humanitarian Award recipient: Elena Grant."

Lena stood up at the applause and walked to the podium. She shook hands with the emcee, then gazed out at the seated crowd.

"What does it mean to be a humanitarian?" she asked. "Vegetarian means someone who eats vegetables. Proletarian means someone who also eats vegetables, just not as many. Although I am an attorney, and have from time to time been referred to as a man-eater, I hope that's not why I am being honored today as a humanitarian."

The audience laughed. Preston applauded.

Lena continued: "We grow up thinking that heroes carry guns and badges, or briefcases and gavels, or stethoscopes and scalpels.

And they do. But sometimes they carry pencils. Sometimes they carry books. Sometimes . . ."

Preston stopped smiling. Lena's voice grew sharper, more brittle.

"They aren't always the easiest people to be around. They are driven by priorities the rest of us may not understand, priorities they aren't always very good at explaining.

"But in their love and gentleness, their honor and selflessness, their oddity, their veracity, their vulnerability, their empathy, they shape the world. They enrich the world. And they make the world proud."

Preston's jaw was taut. His eyes reflected her pain. Tears began to sneak down Lena's face. She ignored them.

"I am proud to accept this award in their honor. We don't always know their names. But we will always remember their gift. Thank you."

Lena returned to her seat. Preston moved to her immediately. The emcee walked back to the podium.

"I. Uh. Thank you, Ms. Grant. Very. Heartfelt."

Lena hurried out the door of the banquet room, pursued by Preston.

"Well," the emcee covered, "I think it's obvious we made the right choice here tonight."

Lena opened her eyes to a rotated world, then realized she was lying on the floor of her apartment. Wolfram guarded one side, Sancho the other. The phone lay nearby. It was ringing.

The trio stared at the phone for many long minutes as it rang. Finally Lena crawled over and lifted the receiver, listened, then closed her eyes.

"Where did they find him?"

She nodded.

"I'll be right there."

She didn't write it down.

CHAPTER 8

No Man

Wolfram walks a crooked path, through the park and down the bank, along the lagoon. Lena follows, one hand on his leash, the other cradling a gray-and-white bundle to her breast.

Past the ambulance.

Past the fire department.

Past the SWAT team.

Past Preston, arms crossed.

Past the park bench, past Sharon, to Oscar, who reads aloud from a Day-Glo three-by-five card: "I was kidnapped and held against my will. I tried to stop him but I couldn't. There was nothing I could do."

"Congratulations," Preston says. "Those are the exact words you need to say to avoid being charged as an accessory. Almost as if an attorney had prepared your statement."

Sharon slips one hand in Oscar's and covers his mouth lovingly with the other.

"As the American philosopher Ralph Waldo Emerson once said, 'Good as is discourse, silence is better, and shames it. The length of the discourse indicates the distance of thought betwixt the speaker and the hearer. If they were at a perfect understanding in any part, no words would be necessary thereon. If at one in all parts, no words would be suffered.'"

"I don't—"

"It means shut up."

"Ahh," Oscar murmurs, nodding into Sharon's palm.

Lena slides gracefully between Oscar and Preston. Wolfram claims his usual place, eclipsing the bench.

"Whose dog is that?" Preston asks, pointing at Wolfram, then thinking better of it and pulling his hand back to safety.

"Whosesoever he wants to be," Lena replies.

"And what are you doing with that puppet?" Preston continues. Lena ignores him this time.

"Where is he?" she asks.

Preston gestures toward the water.

Lena spins.

In the heart of a lake in the heart of a city in the heart of a land in the heart of the world there is an island in the shape of a heart.

Nick is there. But not alone. Cats of all ages and shapes and colors luxuriate in the morning sun. In Nick's arms, a bundle resolves into kittens.

A German shepherd mix bursts through the brush.

Then a Labrador.

Then a beagle.

Watson.

Alonzo.

Fanny.

Pal.

Ricardo.

Rufus.

Grendel.

Annabelle.

Huck.

Then more and more of all shapes and sizes, orbiting Nick in concentric blurs.

"How many?" she asks.

"Every animal in the shelter," Preston replies, then twists around back to Oscar.

"How did he get those animals on the island?"

"Well . . ."

"Don't tell me he walked on water."

"Sort of, he did," Oscar explains. "The channel is only a few yards wide right there and not very deep. So we, he, unloaded the animals and drove the institute van into the lake. It sank, but the top was only an inch below the surface. Then Nick started marching around and around pretending he was playing a musical instrument and the animals began following him and pretty soon they were all marching around and around, the cats and dogs, even the puppies and kittens, and then Nick marched down to the shore and right across the top of the van onto the island and they just followed right after him."

"Was he playing a pipe?" Preston asks.

Oscar ponders.

Lena turns back to the island.

"It was an E-flat cornet," she says.

Nick connects, smiles, stirs. Scrambling kittens around his feet, he leans on the sign.

A policeman and a fireman report to Preston, who orders crossly: "Get those animals off that island."

The world swirls. The colors rush together, remix, then whirl back into place, repainting the day. A thrill surges through her till she can barely breathe. But she laughs anyway.

"You can't do that," she manages to say.

"Why not?" Preston demands.

She collects herself.

"That island is a state wildlife preserve. It takes an executive order from the governor to remove any animals."

"How do you know that?"

"Nick is an expert in wildlife regulation."

Preston turns to the policeman.

"Well, then, get *him* off there at least."

Lena shades her eyes.

Nick points to the sign, then to himself.

"You can't do that either," she announces.

"Why not?" Preston demands again.

"The legislation doesn't distinguish between human animals and other animals. He gets just as much protection as they do."

"How do you know that?"

"We drafted the legislation for one of his wildlife groups. Nick thought it was funny."

Preston storms in a circle, all red in the face and shouting.

"Well, he has to come off there sometime and when he does he's going down for kidnapping or dognapping or catnapping or something."

She tries not to smile, fails.

"You can't do that."

Preston stomps like Rumpelstiltskin.

"Stop saying that!"

Then he sighs.

"Why not?"

Lena manages to look serious.

"Because the judge has already found him incompetent to stand trial. When he comes off the island, he goes back to the institute. But I don't think he's coming off anytime soon."

"Why not?"

"Because someone called the media."

Satellite trucks herd through the narrow lane that encircles the lake. Gaggles of cameras overflow the lakeshore while packs of reporters hustle each other, shouting questions to Nick.

"Looks like every local media outlet in town. Not to mention CNN."

One by one, for the cameras, Nick frames each dog and cat and puppy and kitten. And tells their names. Their stories. Their hopes and dreams.

The cameras capture each one: home free.

Preston makes a funny face.

"What does he want?"

Lena turns to Nick. He places his fist to his forehead, extends his middle finger, and wiggles it subtly, not quite the secret sign of the International Brotherhood of Crustaceans.

Lena turns back to Preston.

"He wants the governor to issue a moratorium on nonmedical animal euthanasia throughout the state and provide additional funding for shelters and adoption programs."

"That's political blackmail. The governor won't agree."

Lena sets her feet wide apart, hands on hips. The salmon merino sweater tied around her neck drapes down her back, rippling in the breeze.

"He'll agree because it's a fucking election year and otherwise he gets to condemn puppies and kittens to death on fucking national television."

Preston revolves, arms whirling, a windmill in a cyclone, shouting, furious, into the air: "Get me the fucking governor. Get me the fucking governor!"

Then he stops. Slowly he turns.

"Tell me," he says.

"What?"

"Tell me that he didn't plan all this from the very beginning."

Lena closes her eyes.

"He doesn't make plans. He has visions."

Preston sighs, nods, releases.

"We never imagine we're not the hero," he says.

Lena kisses Preston gently on the cheek. He waves her down to the lakeshore. She drops Wolfram's leash, threads through reporters and cameras and Ralph and Alice and geese and squirrels and trees and grasses, down to the water's edge.

"You're an animal," she calls.

Nick laughs. The backdrop blurs. Amethyst empties the day of shadow. The topaz sun evaporates the mist, unveiling chalcedony trees and emerald grass. Butterflies hover in sapphire suspension.

Wolfram ambles past in stately solo procession, gliding without hesitation across the water's surface. Nick greets him solemnly with a bow.

Lena peers down through the glimmery beryl reflection, through the mirrored sardonyx purl, through the lake of sunrise fire. The path is there.

And then in the midst, diffracted, refracted, reflected, Nick floats, bobbing softly upside down in the clouds, eyes glowing jasper, transverse but whole.

"It occurs to me," his image expounds, "that if I'm not mentally competent, those divorce papers I signed may not be valid."

Lena opens her mouth to speak. No words. Nick steps out from the bank, lowering one knee to the blazing water.

"I imagine that I will annoy you for as long as we both shall live."

Lena's sheep-caught-in-the-headlights look dissolves. The ritual of joining begins as her right hand slips inside me.

No more questions.

CHAPTER 9

True Minds

All together now.

We love who we imagine.

So love you.

The world through button eyes is a Revelation.

ACKNOWLEDGMENTS

This book and I have benefited from the generous efforts of talented people, especially Liv Blumer, my sagacious and steadfast agent; Bill Blumer, her savvy partner; Sally Arteseros of the sharp pencil and sharper advice; my insightful editor and fiction guru Fred Ramey; and the endlessly energetic Caitlin Hamilton Summie. Thank you all.

I would also like to express my profound thanks to my father and mother, brothers, extended family, old friends and true companions, who have been wonderfully supportive for so many (many) years.

Finally, this story would not have been written if not for the inspiration and encouragement of my aunt, Margaret Norris. The book is dedicated to her memory.